Malory Towers

8

Summer Term

Have you read them all?

Enid Blyton

Malory Towers

Summer Term

Written by Pamela Cox

*Hodder
Children's
Books*

HODDER CHILDREN'S BOOKS

First published in Great Britain in 2009 by Mammoth
This edition published in 2016 by Hodder and Stoughton Ltd

3 5 7 9 10 8 6 4

Written by Pamela Cox

A CIP catalogue record for this book
is available from the British Library.

ISBN 9781444929942

Printed and bound in India by
Manipal Technologies Ltd, Manipal

The paper and board used in this book
are made from wood from responsible sources

Hodder Children's Books
An imprint of
Hachette Children's Group
Part of Hodder and Stoughton
Carmelite House
50 Victoria Embankment
London EC4Y 0DZ

An Hachette UK Company
www.hachette.co.uk

www.hachettechildrens.co.uk

Contents

Contents

Off to Malory Towers

'Where *have* those two girls got to?' asked Mr Rivers impatiently, poking his head out of the car window.

'They will be here any minute,' said his wife calmly. 'Don't forget that they haven't seen each other for a few weeks, so I expect that they have a lot of news to catch up on.'

'Well, they'll have plenty of time to talk on the journey,' said Mr Rivers. 'If we don't leave soon, we shan't reach Malory Towers until after tea.'

Mr and Mrs Rivers were taking their daughter, Felicity, back to her boarding school, Malory Towers, after the holidays, and they had stopped to pick up her friend, Susan, on the way. Felicity had gone into the house to fetch her friend, and she seemed to have been in there for simply ages! At last the front door opened and two laughing, chattering girls emerged. The one with dark, bobbed hair and laughing brown eyes was Felicity, and the other, grey-eyed and snub-nosed, was Susan. Both of them wore the Malory Towers summer uniform, which was an orange and white checked dress, with short sleeves and a crisp white collar, and they looked very smart indeed as they walked arm-in-arm down the path. Behind them came Susan's parents, her mother carrying a night case and her father huffing and puffing as he carried his daughter's trunk to the car.

'My goodness, anyone would think you were going back to school for a whole year, not just a term,' he joked. 'I'm sure that you must have packed the kitchen sink in here.'

The two sets of parents greeted one another, and Mr Rivers got out of the car to help Mr Blake stow the trunk in the boot. Then Susan hugged her parents, the two girls settled themselves in the back seat of the car and they were off – back to Malory Towers.

The school was in Cornwall, and it was a very long drive, but Felicity and Susan had so much to talk about that the first couple of hours simply sped by.

'Won't it be marvellous to see all the others again?' said Susan. 'Good old Pam, and Nora and Julie – not forgetting Jack, of course.'

Jack was their friend Julie's horse, who lived in the stables at Malory Towers during term time, and all the girls were very fond of him indeed.

'I think the summer term is my favourite term of all,' said Felicity excitedly. 'There's so much to do. Picnics, swimming and horse-riding – and I mean to work really hard at my tennis. I'm determined to be picked for one of the teams this term.'

'Me too,' said Susan. 'My word, wouldn't it be super if we were both picked?'

'Super!' agreed Felicity. 'I wonder if there will be any new girls this term.'

'There are sure to be,' Susan said. 'I say, Felicity, I wonder what tricks June and Freddie will have brought back with them this term. Oh, I just can't wait to get back to Malory Towers.'

But, after a stop for lunch, the girls' conversation tailed off, as both of them began to feel a little drowsy from the long car journey. Susan had difficulty in keeping her eyes open, while Felicity actually dropped off to sleep for a little while. But both of them woke up completely when the car rounded a bend in the road and their beloved Malory Towers came into view.

'There it is!' cried Felicity, sitting bolt upright. 'Doesn't it look magnificent, with the sun right behind it?'

Susan was so excited that she couldn't speak, but she nodded her head vigorously, as Mr Rivers turned the car into the long driveway. In front of them was a very long, sleek, expensive-looking car and Felicity said, 'My goodness, just look at that! I wonder who it belongs to?'

'I wouldn't be surprised if it's Amy's,' said Susan. 'It would be just like her to turn up to school in a showy car like that.'

'That's an American car, girls,' Mr Rivers informed them. 'So I doubt very much that it belongs to your friend Amy's family.'

Just then the big car pulled in and a pretty, smartly dressed woman emerged. She opened the back door and a tall, willowy girl with beautifully arranged blonde curls climbed out. Felicity and Susan couldn't see her face, and were bursting with curiosity as she took the

3

woman's arm and walked off gracefully with her.

'Heavens!' said Susan, as she stared after the girl. 'She looked awfully glamorous, didn't she? I wonder which form she'll be in?'

But there was no time to think about that, for, as Mr Rivers brought the car to a halt, Felicity spotted a group of third formers nearby and yelled, 'There are June and Freddie – and I do believe that's Nora!'

'Don't be in such a rush, Felicity,' protested her mother, as everyone got out of the car. 'You have plenty of time in which to chat to your friends, but Daddy and I shan't see you again until half-term.'

'Sorry, Mummy,' said Felicity contritely. 'I shall miss you both, you know. It's just that I get so excited about being back at school and seeing everyone again.'

'I know that you do, dear, and I quite understand,' said Mrs Rivers, smiling. 'Now, here's your night case – and yours, Susan. Have a good term, both of you, and write soon, won't you, Felicity?'

'Of course. Goodbye, Mother! Goodbye, Daddy!' And Felicity hugged each of her parents in turn, then she and Susan waved them off before running to join their friends, all of whom were greeting one another noisily.

'Hallo, June! Hope you've brought some good tricks with you.'

'My word, isn't it super to be back together again?'

'Pam, you're back! Had a good Easter?'

'And here are Felicity and Susan. Who's missing?'

'I haven't seen Amy and Bonnie yet. And I wonder

where Julie is?' said Nora, looking puzzled. 'She usually gets back early so that she can settle Jack in.'

'I bet she's still down at the stables,' said June. 'You know how she fusses over that horse of hers.'

'We'd better go and give our health certificates to Matron and unpack our night cases,' said Felicity. 'By the time we've done that, Julie will probably have satisfied herself that Jack isn't going to pine away if she leaves him for a few hours, and decided to join us.'

But by the time the girls had seen Matron and gone to their dormitory to unpack, there was still no sign of Julie, and even the placid Pam began to look worried, saying anxiously, 'I do hope that she hasn't been taken ill or something. Wouldn't it be dreadful if she missed the beginning of term?'

'I spoke to her on the telephone last week and she sounded perfectly fine then,' said Nora.

'Well, it's no use standing around worrying,' said Susan, sensibly. 'Let's take a walk down to the stables and see if she's there.'

So the group of third formers made their way to the stables, where they found several girls settling their horses in. But Julie and Jack were not among them.

'The stables are all full,' said Felicity. 'So even if Julie turns up with Jack now, there won't be room for him here.'

'How odd!' said Freddie. 'I say, you don't think that Miss Grayling has told Julie that she can't have Jack with her at school any more, do you?'

'The Head wouldn't do that,' said Nora. 'Why, Julie's

always brought him to Malory Towers with her!'

'But it is queer that there isn't a place left for him,' said Susan, frowning, as the girls walked back up to the school. Then a thought occurred to her and she gasped, 'Oh, my goodness! What if something has happened to Jack?'

The others turned pale at the thought and Pam gave a shudder. 'What a dreadful thought! Why, Julie would be simply heartbroken! That horse means the world to her. '

But just then, the girls heard themselves being hailed and they turned to see Julie herself coming towards them, dressed in her riding gear – and the broad smile on her freckled face was enough to tell them at once that Jack was safe and sound. There was another girl with her, who the others hadn't seen before, also dressed in riding clothes, and the third formers looked at her curiously.

'Hallo, everyone!' cried Julie. 'Sorry I'm late, but I've just been stabling Jack at Five Oaks.'

The girls looked a little puzzled at this, for Five Oaks was a riding school not far from Malory Towers, which was run by two old girls, Bill and Clarissa.

'We wondered where you were,' said Felicity. 'But why is Jack staying at Five Oaks, Julie? You always have him here with you.'

'Well, Miss Grayling telephoned me at home the other day and said that more girls than ever were bringing their horses to school with them this term. She said that there wouldn't be room for all of them in the school stables, and would I mind awfully taking Jack to Five Oaks instead. Well, I'm always glad of an excuse to visit Bill and Clarissa, and I know that they'll take jolly good care of Jack, so of course I said yes. Lucy is stabling her horse, Sandy, there as well.'

'Who is Lucy?' asked Nora.

'Oh, of course, I haven't introduced you yet!' exclaimed Julie, taking the new girl's arm. 'This is Lucy Carstairs and she's going to be in our form.'

Felicity, as head-girl of the third form, introduced the others to Lucy, who smiled happily round and said a cheery, 'Hallo, everyone!' She was a tall, slender girl, rather boyish in appearance, with a crop of short dark hair, brilliant blue eyes and a sprinkling of freckles across her nose. She and Julie seemed to have become firm friends, although they hadn't known one another for very long, and June said, 'I suppose we'll have to listen to the two of you gabbling away endlessly about gymkhanas and pony treks and what-not now! That's if we ever get to see you, for I daresay the pair of you will spend all of your spare time at Five Oaks this term.'

'That's the idea,' said Lucy, with a grin. 'I simply can't be away from Sandy for too long, or I'll just pine away.'

'Well, I've heard of horses pining for their owners, but never an owner pining for her horse!' said Felicity, with a chuckle. 'Anyway, welcome to Malory Towers, Lucy. I hope you'll settle in and be happy here.'

'I'm sure that I shall,' said Lucy, with her ready smile, and the others warmed to her at once.

'Well, it looks as if Julie has found a special friend of her own,' said Felicity to Susan, as the girls made their way down to the swimming-pool, which they were eager to show off to Lucy. 'Which is a very good thing. I know that she's always had Jack but, even though he's lovely, you can't really have a conversation with a horse.'

'Well, you can, but they tend to be pretty one-sided,' laughed Susan. 'I know what you mean, though. Julie gets along well with everyone, but it's so nice to have a special person to share jokes and secrets with. We're all paired up now, aren't we? There's June and Freddie, Pam and Nora, Amy and Bonnie, Julie and Lucy – oh, and not forgetting the two of us, of course!'

It was a glorious day, and the swimming-pool, of which Malory Towers was justly proud, was at its finest. The pool was hollowed out of rocks and filled naturally by the sea, and as she watched the sun glinting on the surface of the water, Felicity longed to plunge in. So did June, who said, 'It's so warm today. A dip in the pool would just cool me down nicely.'

'Jump in, then,' said Freddie, her eyes alight with mischief. 'I bet you daren't!'

Of course, it simply wasn't in June's nature to refuse a dare, and before the others realised what was happening, she had jumped into the pool fully clothed, making a terrific splash and sending a shower of water over Freddie, who was standing nearest.

'June!' cried Felicity, between shock and laughter. 'Come out of there at once! My goodness, you'll get into the most terrific row from Matron if she sees you in those wet clothes! Freddie, you're absolutely soaked too.'

Lucy was staring at June as if she couldn't believe her eyes and, seeing her expression, Nora laughed and said, 'June's a real dare-devil. You never know what she'll do next, but she certainly livens things up in the third form.'

'I'll just bet she does,' said Lucy, beginning to laugh as well. 'My goodness, I'm so glad that my parents decided to send me to Malory Towers. I've only been here a short while, but I know already that I'm going to love it.'

'Glad to hear it,' said Felicity. 'I've a feeling you're going to fit in here just fine, Lucy.' Then she gave a squeal, as June, who was still fooling around in the swimming-pool, sent a spray of water in her direction. Leaping back she yelled, 'That's quite enough, June. I don't want to get into trouble on my first day back, even if you do.'

'Yes, come on out now,' said Susan. 'It'll be time for tea soon, and you can't go into the dining-room looking like a drowned rat!'

Grinning, June climbed out of the pool, shaking herself to get rid of some of the water, and Pam said, 'You remind me of my dog, Monty! He shakes himself like that when he's had a bath.'

'Well, I feel as if I've had a shower!' complained Freddie, who had taken her socks off and was trying to wring the water out of them. 'You beast, June! Now I shall have to get changed too.'

'You two will have to get out of your riding gear as well,' said Felicity to Julie and Lucy. 'Let's be quick, for I don't want to be late for tea. I'm starving!'

'And let's hope we don't bump into Matron, or any

of the mistresses on the way back,' said Susan.

The girls didn't, but they did have the misfortune to meet a particularly unpleasant fifth former, Eleanor Banks, and she turned her nose up in disgust as she spotted the two dripping-wet girls. Eleanor had joined the fifth form last term, and had lost no time in making herself unpopular with the younger girls. She had a very cold, haughty manner and that, along with her pale colouring and silvery-blonde hair, had led June to nickname her the Ice Queen. Somehow this had got back to Eleanor, and there was no love lost between June and her at all!

'What on earth have you third formers been up to?' Eleanor asked now, her cold stare fixed on June.

'I've been up to my neck in water, Eleanor,' answered June cheekily, quite unabashed by the older girl's cool manner. 'And poor Freddie here caught the backlash.'

'June slipped and fell into the pool,' said Felicity hastily, seeing two spots of angry red appear on Eleanor's pale cheeks. 'She's just off to get changed now.'

Eleanor didn't believe that June had fallen into the pool by accident for a moment. The wretched girl was always acting the goat! But since she couldn't prove anything, she was unable to dish out a punishment, which made her feel extremely disappointed. Instead she had to content herself with a few sharp words. 'Well, hurry up about it,' she snapped. 'Or you'll be late for tea. And you two,' she turned to Julie and Lucy now. 'Change out of those riding clothes before you go into the dining-room. Come on, now – shake a leg!'

Then Eleanor squealed, for June suddenly shook her head violently, sending drops of water all over the fifth former.

'How dare you!' she gasped, pulling a handkerchief from her pocket and dabbing at her dress. 'Just look what you've done!'

'But you told me to shake my head,' said June, staring innocently at Eleanor, as the rest of the third formers struggled to hide their smiles.

'I said shake a *leg*,' said Eleanor, through gritted teeth. 'As you very well know!'

'Oh, did you?' said June. 'Sorry, Eleanor. I must have some water in my ears.'

Eleanor glared angrily at the girl, but at that moment someone called her name and she turned to see Bella Coombes, head of the fifth form, beckoning her over.

'Saved by the Bella!' quipped June, as Eleanor stalked away, and the others laughed.

'You'd better watch out for Eleanor, June,' warned Pam. 'She's always had it in for you, and she'll be even worse now.'

'Pooh!' said June scornfully. 'The Ice Queen will never get the better of me!'

'Was that the Head Girl?' Lucy asked Julie, as they made their way back to the school.

'No, Eleanor just *thinks* that she's Head Girl,' answered Julie drily. 'Mean beast! She came to Malory Towers last term because her parents went abroad. Her aunt and uncle live near Five Oaks, so she stays with them during the holidays.'

'If you ask me, Eleanor's parents went abroad to get away from her,' said June 'And I can't say that I blame them. Still, I daresay that her pitiful attempts to make trouble for me will provide us with some amusement this term.'

'I daresay they will,' said Felicity, grinning. What a super term this was going to be. Oh, it *was* good to be back at school!

The new girls

There was a surprise in store for the third formers as they poured noisily into their dormitory in the North Tower. Amy and Bonnie were there, unpacking, and with them was another new girl! She was talking to Bonnie when the girls entered, and had her back to the door, but Felicity and Susan recognised her at once as the willowy blonde girl who had been in the big American car.

Then she turned, and the third formers gasped in astonishment. For her face was almost identical to Lucy's! It was the same shape, had the same bright blue eyes and the same wide, generous mouth. But where Lucy looked boyish, this girl, with her blonde curls and sophisticated air, was very feminine indeed. And while Lucy strode briskly, the new girl was so graceful that she seemed almost to glide as she moved across to her bed.

The third formers greeted Amy and Bonnie, then Bonnie gestured towards the new girl and said in her soft voice, 'Have you met Esme yet?'

'No, we haven't,' said Felicity, smiling at the new girl. 'Welcome to the third form, Esme. Lucy, you never told us that you had a twin!'

But Lucy was looking every bit as startled as the others,

and not at all pleased. She said rather curtly now, 'She's not my twin. In fact, we aren't even sisters. Esme and I are cousins.'

'Golly!' exclaimed Freddie, looking from one to the other. 'The likeness is quite astonishing!'

'Our mothers are twins.' Esme spoke for the first time, and the others were surprised to hear her American accent. Most of the girls had never heard one before, except in films, and it was quite fascinating to listen to. She was rather fascinating to look at too, and seemed a lot more grown-up than the other girls. She was wearing lipstick, Felicity realised disapprovingly, and she had mascara on her eyelashes too. But how silly of her to want to wear make-up, when she was naturally so very pretty anyway.

Lucy was obviously very put out by her cousin's arrival and asked rather brusquely, 'What are you doing here, Esme?'

'Gee, it's nice to see you too, cousin,' drawled the girl, raising her eyebrows. 'I'm here for the same reason as you, I imagine. To get an education.'

'Surely they have schools in America,' said Lucy sharply, and the listening girls goggled, quite taken aback at her rudeness. Felicity looked at her hard and wondered if the first, favourable impression that Lucy had made on her had been false.

Esme, however, didn't seem at all upset, and merely replied calmly, 'Sure they do – very good ones. But Mother missed England, so we moved back here last month and we're going to be staying for a while.'

Lucy looked absolutely furious at this and snapped, 'Well, the school you went to in America can't have been *that* good, for you're a year older than me and should be in the fourth form, not the third.'

The third formers drank all this in avidly, casting sidelong glances at Esme to see how she was taking this. And they had to admire her composure when she refused to rise to Lucy's baiting and said matter-of-factly, 'Miss Grayling and Mother decided between them that it would be best to spend my first term in the third form, seeing as I've been studying different things from you girls. If all goes well, I'll go up into a higher form next term. So I guess you'll just have to get used to having me around for a while, Lucy.'

As though she didn't trust herself to speak, Lucy turned away from her cousin abruptly and began to get changed. The third formers were simply bursting with curiosity as to what could be behind the hostility between the cousins, but of course they were far too well-mannered to pry.

Lucy wasn't the only one who wasn't very impressed with the new girl, for Amy also looked down her rather long nose at her, Felicity noticed. She felt quite sorry for Esme, who seemed very easy-going and good-natured, and asked, 'How long have you lived in America?'

'About four years,' answered Esme. 'You see, my father's American and he met my mother when he was working over here. After the two of them married, they settled in England. They wanted to live here for good, but . . . well, things just didn't work out, so we all moved to

America. I loved it there, but Mother always felt homesick. She was so happy to come back home.'

'How is Aunt Maggie?' asked Lucy, unexpectedly, her expression softening a little.

'She's fine,' answered Esme. 'Just fine. And Aunt Janet?'

'She's very well, thank you,' said Lucy stiffly.

There was an awkward little silence, which was broken by the sound of a bell ringing, and Nora cried, 'Teatime! Thank goodness, I'm so hungry I could eat a horse.'

'Don't say that in front of Julie and Lucy,' laughed Pam. 'They'll have visions of you stalking Jack and Sandy with a knife and fork!'

'Gee, do you still have Sandy?' said Esme, turning to her cousin. 'He was little more than a foal when I left England.'

'Yes,' answered Lucy. 'He's stabled just along the road from here.'

'It'll be nice to see him again,' Esme said, as the third formers began to make their way down the stairs. 'I always had a soft spot for Sandy.'

Lucy didn't look thrilled at the idea of Esme getting too close to her beloved Sandy, and before she could dish out another rebuff to her cousin, Pam asked hastily, 'Do you ride, Esme?'

'Not very well,' answered the girl, with a rueful smile. 'I like horses, but I get a little nervous when I'm in the saddle. It always seems such an awfully long way from the ground!'

The others laughed at this, all except Lucy, who scowled fiercely at her cousin. Julie felt a little disappointed in her.

Lucy had seemed so happy and friendly at first, but since Esme's arrival she had gone all sulky and moody, making everyone else feel rather uncomfortable. And Julie couldn't see any reason for it. Because, although Esme was very different from the other girls, she seemed perfectly pleasant and friendly. As though sensing that Julie was unhappy, Lucy took her arm and pulled her aside from the others as they entered the dining-room.

'I'm sorry,' she said contritely. 'I didn't mean to cause an atmosphere, truly I didn't.'

There was an earnest expression in her blue eyes, and suddenly Lucy looked much more like the nice, fun-loving girl Julie had been introduced to at Five Oaks.

'But I don't understand why you're so hard on Esme,' said Julie. 'She is your cousin, after all.'

Lucy bit her lip and said, 'I don't want to say too much at the moment, but . . . well, there was a big falling out between our families a few years ago, and the two of us haven't seen one another, or spoken, since.'

Julie felt quite saddened by this, thinking what a lot of unhappiness was caused when families rowed. But the two cousins both seemed like good-hearted girls, and perhaps being at school together would give them the chance to patch up their differences. Lucy certainly seemed determined to brush her cares aside now, and, pinning a bright smile on her face, she clapped Julie on the shoulder and said, 'Don't take any notice of me! As Esme said, she's here for a while and I'll just have to get used to it. I certainly don't intend to let her spoil my time at

Malory Towers, or the fun that you and I are going to have together with Jack and Sandy.'

'That's more like it!' said Julie happily, returning the girl's smile. 'Now come on, let's go and get some tea before the others polish everything off.'

First-night suppers at Malory Towers were always marvellous, and tonight was no exception. There was cold chicken, potato salad and big juicy tomatoes, followed by the most delicious apple pie with cream. Jugs of ice-cold lemonade stood on the tables, and the girls helped themselves to big glasses as they ate.

'Gee, this food sure is good!' said Esme, tucking into her second slice of apple pie.

'Wizard!' said Susan, doing likewise.

'*Wizard?*' repeated Esme, looking puzzled. 'What does that mean?'

'It means super, smashing, first-rate, top-hole,' explained June, with a grin. 'Or, as you Americans would say, *wunnerful*!'

'Esme's not American,' protested Freddie, as the others laughed. 'She was born in England and spent most of her life here, so she's English.'

'Well, gee, she sure *sounds* American,' said Nora in a fine imitation of Esme's accent. Everyone laughed, and Esme said with a grin, 'That was just wizard, Nora.'

Then the third formers began to point out various girls and mistresses to the two cousins, Felicity saying, 'That's Kay Foster, the Head Girl, and the big girl next to her is Amanda Chartelow, the games captain. They're both good sorts, though Amanda has a bit of a temper at times.'

'Yes, but she's hot-tempered rather than bad-tempered,' said Susan. 'And she only gets really angry with people who are lazy, or don't make an effort when it comes to games.'

Esme looked rather dismayed at this and said, 'Do you play a lot of games here, then?'

'You bet,' said Pam. 'The tennis-courts are simply marvellous. If you like, I'll take you to see them after tea.'

'No, thanks, Pam,' said Esme, with a laugh. 'I'm afraid I'm not very interested in games or sports of any kind. I have better things to do!'

She sounded quite scornful and the others felt a little annoyed, June asking with deceptive sweetness, 'And just how do you spend your valuable time, Esme? Painting your nails? Dear me, I'd love to be a fly on the wall when you tell Amanda that you can't come to tennis practice because you're busy doing your hair! My goodness, she'll drag you out on to that tennis-court with your hair curlers in!'

Lucy and one or two others laughed rather unkindly, while Esme looked taken aback and turned red. 'I didn't mean to cause any offence,' she said. 'It's just that at my old school, in America, we didn't have to go in for games if we didn't want to.'

'Well, I'm afraid you'll have to at Malory Towers, Esme, whether you like it or not,' said Felicity. 'Everyone does.'

'Unless you can find a way of getting out of them,' put in Bonnie. She was a very small, rather doll-like girl, with

19

big eyes and soft brown curls. But her appearance was deceptive, for Bonnie was a determined and resourceful character, who always found the most ingenious ways to get out of doing anything that she didn't want to do.

Esme liked Bonnie and her friend, Amy, and felt that she had a lot more in common with them than these other, rather hearty English girls. They were nice, feminine girls who took pride in their appearance and could think of more important things than chasing balls around, or plunging into an icy-cold swimming-pool! But although Bonnie seemed friendly enough, Amy was a bit stuck-up and rather cool towards her. Esme had caught the girl giving her one or two cold, haughty stares and wondered what she could possibly have done to offend Amy. But maybe that was the way she looked at everyone – after all, with a nose that long how could she *help* but look down it at people?

In fact, Amy had decided that Esme was rather vulgar and common, with that dreadful American drawl and that awful make-up. Didn't she realise how cheap she made herself look? She was surprised and displeased with Bonnie for paying the girl so much attention, and looked very unhappy now as Esme turned to Bonnie and began to talk about fashions. This was a subject close to Amy's heart, and normally she would have joined in, but her dislike of the new girl stopped her, and, instead, she sat there pushing the food around her plate, a scowl on her face.

'Just look at Amy,' whispered June to Freddie. 'She's

not at all pleased to see Bonnie making friends with Esme. I suppose she thinks that Esme is beneath her notice.'

'It hasn't taken Amy long to get back to her old, snobbish self again!' said Freddie. 'I did think, for a while, that she was going to forget her stuck-up ways and become one of us, but now that she has got over the shock of finding out that her mother's family isn't as grand as she believed, she is just as bad as she was before!'

Just then, plump little Mam'zelle Dupont, one of the school's two French mistresses bustled across. She had just arrived back from her holiday in France, and looked relaxed and happy as she sat down at the head of the table, crying, 'Ah, how good it is to see you all back again! Well rested and ready to work hard at your French.'

'Heavens, Mam'zelle, we shan't have any time for French this term,' said June, with a wicked grin. 'We shall be far too busy with other things. Swimming, for one.'

'And horse-riding,' put in Julie.

'And tennis,' said Felicity. 'Really, Mam'zelle, I don't know if we will have time to do any work at all!'

'Ah, you tease me, bad girls!' said Mam'zelle, smiling indulgently as she piled her plate with food. 'But I see we have two new girls – twins!'

'They aren't twins, Mam'zelle,' explained Pam. 'Lucy and Esme are cousins.'

'But they are so alike!' exclaimed Mam'zelle, scrutinising the two new girls so closely that they both became quite red with embarrassment. 'Yet, in some ways, not alike.' There was a slightly stern note in her tone, for she now saw that Esme was wearing make-up – and Mam'zelle did not approve of such things. But then the girl said something to Nora, and Mam'zelle, realising that she was American, softened towards her. American girls were different, thought the French mistress, philosophically. They seemed to grow up faster than English girls, and had different ideas. Once this Esme had been under the influence of Malory Towers and the dear third formers for a while, she would learn English ways and become a proper schoolgirl.

This was exactly what Felicity was hoping, too. A thought occurred to her and she said to Susan, 'Esme's arrival means that we aren't all neatly paired up any more, for she is the odd one out now.'

'Golly, yes, I hadn't thought of that,' said Susan. 'Well, she seems quite nice, although she's so different from the rest of us. We shall all have to do our best to see that she's not left out.' She looked across to where the new girl was chatting to Bonnie, and noticed that Lucy was watching too, a discontented frown on her face. 'I wonder why Lucy and Esme dislike one another so?' she said.

'Perhaps we'll find out one day,' said Felicity. 'I just hope that they manage to rub along together all right, and don't make everyone else feel uncomfortable.'

The two new girls managed to avoid one another in the common-room that evening. Lucy and Julie sat in a corner together, chattering nineteen-to-the-dozen about horses, while Esme joined the others.

'Gosh, I'm tired,' said Nora, with a yawn. 'I don't know

why the first day back at school is always so exhausting, for we don't do any work, but it always wears me out.'

'Well, the bell will be going for bedtime soon,' said Susan.

'But it's only eight o'clock,' said Esme, in surprise. 'That seems awfully early to go to bed.'

'We only go at eight on the first evening,' explained Pam. 'Because we're all supposed to be jolly tired after our long journeys. Normally we stay up until nine.'

'Gee, we went up much later than that at my school in America,' said Esme. 'I'll never be able to get to sleep at nine o'clock!'

'Oh yes you will!' Felicity told her, with a grin. 'Once you've played a few games out in the fresh air.'

'Yes, a few lengths of the swimming-pool tomorrow will tire you out,' said Susan. 'And if that doesn't do the trick, a few sets of tennis ought to help.'

Poor Esme looked horrified, and the others laughed at her.

'Don't worry, Esme,' said Freddie. 'Amanda will understand if you tell her that you haven't played much sport before, and she won't expect too much of you to begin with. In fact, she'll probably arrange some extra coaching sessions for you.'

Esme wasn't sure whether Freddie was joking or not – gee, she sure hoped that she was! Her mother had been so keen for her to come to Malory Towers, because she had said that Esme had begun to forget that she was half-English, and was becoming 'too American'. But if being English meant having to get hot, sweaty and untidy chasing a ball around, or getting her carefully set hair ruined in a pool, then Esme would rather be American any day! And then there was Lucy. Esme had got the shock of her life when she had realised that the cousin she hadn't seen for years was here too – and in the same form. She began to wonder if she would ever fit in at Malory Towers – certainly not if Lucy had anything to do with it!

A hard time for Esme

Felicity watched, torn between amusement and exasperation, as Esme got ready for breakfast the following morning. The girl had insisted on sleeping with curlers in her hair last night, even though the task of putting them in had had to be accomplished in darkness. Felicity was extremely strict about putting the lights out on time, and flatly refused to break the rule except in an emergency.

'But this *is* an emergency,' Esme had wailed. 'How am I going to make a good impression on our form mistress if my hair's a mess?'

'My dear Esme, I can assure you that Miss Peters won't give a fig for how your hair looks,' Felicity had informed the new girl, grinning to herself in the darkness at the thought of how the forthright, no-nonsense Miss Peters was likely to react to Esme. The mistress had no time at all for what she called 'frills and fancies', and Felicity could see trouble ahead for the girl.

Now Esme was standing in front of a big mirror, carefully removing the curlers and patting each blonde curl into place.

But Felicity's amused smile turned to a frown as Esme began applying lipstick, and she said to Susan, 'Now that's something that most definitely won't make a good impression on Miss Peters! And she's put that awful black stuff on her eyelashes as well.'

A couple of terms ago, Felicity would have been a little diffident about tackling Esme, for she had lacked confidence and been a little shy about expressing her opinions, always rather afraid of offending others. But two terms as head-girl of the third form had changed her. Felicity's belief in herself had grown, along with her confidence, and now she marched up to the new girl, saying forthrightly, 'Esme, you can't go downstairs with that stuff on your face! Wipe it off at once!'

'Why?' asked the girl, turning to face Felicity in surprise. 'What's wrong with it?'

'Well, for one thing, it looks simply awful,' said Felicity. 'I can't think why you want to go around looking as if you're about twenty, when you look perfectly fine just as you are. And, for another thing, Miss Peters will certainly send you out of the room to wash it off. The girls at Malory Towers don't wear make-up.'

'I can see that,' said Esme, a little stung by Felicity's words. 'You would all look so much more glamorous if you did.'

'We're not here to look glamorous,' Felicity told her sharply. 'We're here to learn, and play games and have fun. Perhaps you should try it, Esme.'

But Esme shook her head, saying in her lazy drawl, 'You and your friends are a nice bunch, Felicity, but I'm not like you. And – don't take offence – I don't *want* to be like you.

So I guess Malory Towers is going to have to take me as I am – and so is your Miss Peters.'

Felicity opened her mouth to argue, then changed her mind. What was the point? None of them could turn Esme into an English schoolgirl. Only Esme herself could do that – if she decided that she wanted to. And Felicity couldn't force the girl to wipe her make-up off, but Miss Peters could – and would! Esme was going to have to learn the hard way.

Immediately after breakfast, Esme, Lucy and the other new girls had to go and see Miss Grayling, the Head mistress. Esme felt very nervous, for she hadn't yet spoken to Miss Grayling. But she had seen her briefly in the dining-room, and had thought that she looked most distinguished and rather grand. So she was pleasantly surprised when, on entering the Head's study, Miss Grayling greeted the new girls with a warm smile. The words that she spoke made a great impression on Esme, and Lucy too. The Head began by welcoming each girl individually and asking her name and form. Then her expression became more serious as she addressed the whole group.

'I would like you all to listen carefully,' she said, her clear blue eyes moving from one girl to the next. 'For what I have to say is very important. One day you will leave this school and go out into the world as young women. You should take with you eager minds, kind hearts and a will to help. You should take with you a good understanding, a sense of responsibility, and show others that you are women to be loved, trusted and respected. These are all qualities that you will be able to learn at Malory Towers – if you *wish* to learn them.'

Miss Grayling paused, and every girl in the room felt that the Head was speaking to her and her alone.

'I do not count as our successes those who have passed exams and won scholarships, though they are great achievements. I count as our successes those who are good-hearted and kind, sensible and trustworthy. Responsible women, on whom others can rely. Our failures are those who do not learn those things during their years here.'

All of the new girls listened intently, every one of them inspired by the Head's words and determined that they were going to be one of Malory Towers' successes. Even vain, silly Esme, who left Miss Grayling's study with her pretty head in a whirl as, for the first time, she began seriously to consider that perhaps there were more important things in life than one's appearance. Goodness, perhaps her transformation into an English schoolgirl was beginning already!

But Esme still had a long way to go, and she soon fell foul of Miss Peters. She and Lucy, along with three new girls from other towers, hung back while the others chose their seats. The coveted desks at the back of the class went to the leaders of the form – Felicity, Susan and June. Freddie slipped in next to June, while Pam, Nora and Julie took the row in front of them. Soon only the new girls were left standing. There was an empty seat next to Julie, and Rita, a new South Tower girl, moved towards it, only to receive a ferocious glare from Julie. So poor Rita hastily backed away, and Julie beckoned Lucy across.

'Thanks,' said Lucy gratefully, slipping into the seat. 'I was awfully afraid that I wouldn't be able to sit next to you.'

Esme was left with a seat in the hated front row, right under Miss Peters's sharp eyes, but she took it without complaining, pretending not to notice the slightly pitying look that her cousin gave her. In fact, Esme didn't mind at all being in the front row, for it would be all the easier for her to make an impression on Miss Peters.

Alas for Esme! She certainly did make an impression on the mistress, but it wasn't a good one.

The third formers got to their feet as Miss Peters strode in. She was a rather mannish young woman, with short hair and a rosy complexion, and Esme couldn't help staring at her, for she had never seen anyone quite like her before. Miss Peters always looked rather uncomfortable in the smart blouse and skirt that she wore while teaching, and felt far more at home in her riding gear. She smiled round at her class now and said, 'Good morning, girls. Please sit down.'

The class sat obediently and the mistress said, 'I see that we have a few new girls, and I would like you all to stand up, one by one, and introduce yourselves to me and to the class.'

Rita, from South Tower, stood up first, her knees trembling, for it was quite nerve-wracking to stand up in front of all these girls. Her voice quavering a little, she introduced herself quickly, then sat down again, rather red in the face. It was Esme's turn next, and she was determined to make a better showing than Rita had. Eagerly she got to her feet and began confidently, 'Hallo, Miss Peters. Hallo, third formers. I'm Esme Walters and –'

'One moment!' Miss Peters interrupted her, looking hard at the girl. 'Esme, did you have jam for breakfast this morning?'

'Jam?' repeated the girl, puzzled. 'No, Miss Peters.'

'Then what is that red stuff all around your mouth?' asked the mistress.

Esme blushed a fiery red – as red as her lipstick – as muffled laughter ran round the classroom, and Miss Peters said firmly, 'Quiet, please! Esme, I am waiting for an answer.'

'It's lipstick, Miss Peters,' answered the girl.

'Lipstick!' repeated the mistress, sounding quite horrified. 'Go and wash it off at once, please. And is that mascara on your eyelashes? I thought so! Remove that as well. Quickly, now!'

Esme was every bit as horrified as Miss Peters, but one glance at the mistress's grimly determined face told her that it would be useless to protest, so she walked from the room, head down so that she didn't have to face the mocking glances of the rest of the girls.

She went into the nearest bathroom, where it took her a few minutes to remove her make-up. And how much younger and prettier she looked without it! Esme didn't see it like that at all, though, and thought that she looked very plain indeed. Almost as plain as these jolly English girls!

She felt rather humiliated too, certain that Lucy and a few of the others would crow over her. Gee, maybe she *should* have listened to Felicity after all!

The class was busy making out timetables when Esme returned, and everyone looked up as the door opened.

'Much better!' said Miss Peters approvingly. 'Sit down now, Esme, and begin copying the timetable from the blackboard.'

The girls thought that Esme looked much better too, and her resemblance to Lucy was much more striking now that the make-up had been removed. Felicity opened her mouth to say as much to Susan, but Miss Peters caught her eye and she hastily shut it again. The third-form mistress certainly didn't intend to stand any nonsense this term!

Nor did Miss Maxwell, the games mistress, and poor Esme found herself in hot water again during tennis practice that afternoon. Miss Maxwell partnered the girl with June, and the two of them played doubles against Felicity and Susan. The games mistress was pleased to see that Esme had a graceful style and a good eye – but unless the ball was placed where she could reach it easily, she made no effort to hit it, and refused to exert herself at all. This did not please June, who was a ferociously competitive player, chasing after every ball, even when it seemed impossible to reach.

'Esme!' she cried in exasperation, as one of Felicity's serves whizzed right past her. 'If only you'd run to the baseline you could have got that one back!'

'Gee, keep your hair on, June!' said Esme with a

comical expression. 'It's only a game!'

Unfortunately for Esme, this was the worst thing that she could have said, for June hated to be beaten at anything. Felicity and Susan were both very good players, while June was outstanding at tennis. Had June's partner been Freddie, who also played well, they would have stood a very good chance of winning. As it was, June felt that she was taking on her two opponents single-handed, and she soon grew hot, out of breath and irritable. Felicity took pity on her and sent a few easy shots Esme's way, which the girl managed to hit back. But June knew that Felicity was going easy on her, and that just made her even crosser.

Amanda Chartelow, who joined Miss Maxwell to watch the match, wasn't impressed with the new girl either.

'My word, June just gets better and better!' she said, a note of pride in her voice, for she had coached June herself. 'Did you see how powerful that serve was, Miss Maxwell? And just look at the way she's putting herself at full stretch to reach that return.'

'Felicity and Susan are coming along very well, too,' said the games mistress. 'There really are some very talented players in the third form this term.'

'And one extremely *un*talented one!' said Amanda, glaring in Esme's direction. 'Now there's a candidate for some extra coaching, if ever I saw one.'

'The pity is that she could be quite promising, if only she would make the effort,' said Miss Maxwell with a frown. 'She places the ball well, and her service is good.'

After watching Esme for a few moments, Amanda had

32

to agree, and said, 'But she's dreadfully lazy! She's leaving June to do all the hard work.'

And one thing Amanda had no patience with was laziness. She knew Esme's sort – she was the kind of girl who didn't like exerting herself in case it made her hair untidy, or her face red. Well, Amanda vowed, she was jolly well going to make the new girl skip around a bit and think about something other than her appearance!

So when the quartet of third formers came off the court, the games captain had a few words for each of them.

'Jolly well played, Felicity and Susan!' she said, in her loud voice. 'I must say, the two of you have improved no end. You must have been practising like anything in the hols.'

'We were,' said Felicity, thrilled at the bigger girl's words. 'I say, Amanda, do you think there's any chance of either of us playing for the team this term?'

'Well, I can't make any promises,' said Amanda, smiling at Felicity's eagerness. 'But you're both in with a chance, that much I will say!'

Then she turned to June and said, 'The same goes for you. You have it in you to do really well for the school if you put your mind to it.'

June grinned and thanked Amanda rather off-handedly, but inwardly she was very pleased indeed. She might appear don't-careish, but Malory Towers was beginning to have an effect on June, and she felt a sense of pride in it, and was starting to think that she might like to give something back.

'As for you,' began Amanda, looking rather sternly at Esme, 'I've never seen such a hopeless display in my life! What's your name?'

'Esme Walters,' answered Esme, looking rather afraid of this big, outspoken girl.

'Well, Esme, you're going to have to play up a bit if you want to get into one of the teams,' said Amanda crisply.

Esme didn't have the slightest interest in getting into one of the teams, but somehow she couldn't quite bring herself to say so to Amanda, who looked as if she breathed, slept and ate games! Amanda was quite unaware of Esme's complete absence of enthusiasm, for her imagination was not a lively one and it was quite unthinkable to her that anyone could fail to share her passion for games. So she said bracingly, 'I'm holding a coaching session on Monday afternoon. Come along and we'll see if we can get you up to scratch.'

With that she strode off, leaving Felicity and Susan struggling to contain their smiles at Esme's expression of dismay. June was not so restrained and said with an unkind laugh, 'Now do you see where your vanity has got you, Esme? If only you had made a bit more effort, Amanda wouldn't have singled you out like that. As it is, she's going to have her eye on you from now on. I hope for your sake that you make a better showing at swimming tomorrow, or you'll be down for extra coaching at the pool too!'

Poor Esme groaned inwardly, for she didn't like swimming any better than tennis. Oh dear, what a difficult term this was going to be!

Settling in

As the first week of term sped by, the two new girls settled down in their own ways. Lucy was moderately good at most of her lessons, and well behaved enough not to attract any unwelcome attention from the teachers, most of the time. However, when she became bored she had a habit of daydreaming about riding off across the fields on Sandy, and this earned her a ticking off from Miss Peters and the stern Mam'zelle Rougier on several occasions. On the whole, though, Lucy was very happy at Malory Towers and enjoyed life there. She and Julie got on very well indeed, and, as Five Oaks was only a few minutes walk from the school, the two of them managed to slip over there every day to check on their beloved horses and enjoy a ride together.

Life was not so easy for Esme, however. The girl wasn't stupid, by any means, but the lessons at Malory Towers were very different from what she had been used to in America and she sometimes struggled to keep up with the others. Rather surprisingly, the one thing she excelled at was English. Miss Hibbert took the third formers for this lesson, and although Esme's way of pronouncing certain words drove the mistress mad at times, she produced some very good written work.

'I find it very strange that the only girl who managed to get top marks for her essay this week is someone who has spent the last few years living in a different country,' Miss Hibbert had said at the beginning of one lesson. 'Very well done indeed, Esme.'

'Jolly good show, Esme,' Felicity had said after class, clapping the girl on the back, and Esme had turned red with pleasure.

She turned red during games as well – but from exertion, not from pleasure! Amanda Chartelow had kept her word and been most strict about ensuring that Esme attended her extra coaching. Amanda played a set against Esme herself, but instead of feeling honoured – as the others told her that she should – the girl just felt extremely nervous and made some silly mistakes. The games captain pointed these out to her in great detail, then proceeded to run her ragged! Poor Esme limped off the tennis-court at the end of the set with blistered feet, a red face and a very poor opinion of her ability! Nor did she fare much better at swimming. She wasn't afraid of the water – so long as she stayed in the shallow end – but complained that it ruined her hair. And when Felicity suggested that she wear a bathing cap, Esme didn't care for that idea either, as it would flatten her carefully set curls. The others found it very funny to watch Esme desperately trying to keep her head above the water as she swam around in the shallow end, and it soon became quite a sport among them to try to get the girl's hair wet.

Esme was quite popular with the third formers, but felt

that she had little in common with most of them. The two she felt most akin to were Amy and Bonnie, but although Bonnie seemed to like her, Amy showed all too plainly that she had no time for Esme. Which was a shame, for Esme felt that life at this no-nonsense English school would be much easier to bear if she had like-minded friends to talk to.

She spoke about it to Bonnie in the common-room one evening, saying with a sigh, 'Felicity and the others are really nice girls, but they're just not my type somehow.'

'Well, I don't mind if you want to tag along with Amy and me,' said Bonnie, who liked the good-natured Esme and felt a little sorry for her.

'You might not mind, but I can't see Amy being too keen on the idea,' said Esme glumly.

'Oh, it's easy enough to get round Amy,' said Bonnie airily. 'All you have to do is flatter her, admire her and show her that you look up to her. She simply adores that sort of thing.'

'Really?' said Esme doubtfully, thinking that it sounded too simple to be true.

'Really,' said Bonnie firmly. 'Look, here she comes now. Try it and you'll see that I'm right.'

Amy walked over to the two girls, smiling at Bonnie, but ignoring Esme. The early evening sun shining through the common-room window glinted on her golden hair and Esme exclaimed admiringly, 'How lovely and shiny your hair is, Amy! I do wish that mine would gleam like that.'

Amy looked at the girl in surprise, then she gave a

faint, pleased smile and said, 'You should brush it a hundred times every night before you go to bed. That's what I do.'

Esme nodded, staring at the girl intently as though she were hanging off her every word, and said, 'I shall try that. You know, Amy, I think that you and Bonnie are far and away the prettiest girls in the form. And the nicest.'

Amy unbent still more, her smile widening as she said, 'Why, thank you, Esme.'

Bonnie's eyes danced as she picked up the sewing she was working on and she said to Amy, 'Esme was just saying that she doesn't really feel as if she fits in with the others.'

'Awfully hearty, aren't they?' said Amy, wrinkling her nose.

'Yes, that's exactly the word to describe them!' said Esme. 'But my mother wants me to be a proper English schoolgirl, just like them, and I don't think I can be.'

'Well, Amy and I are English schoolgirls and we are *nothing* like them,' said Bonnie.

'That's very true!' said Esme, looking thoughtful. 'You are just as English as they are, but in a different way – a *good* way. I wouldn't mind becoming more English if it meant that I could be like you two. If only you could teach me.'

'We *can* teach you!' said Amy, looking excited all of a sudden. 'We can teach you how to say "wonderful" instead of "wunnerful", and "twenty" instead of "twenny".'

'And how to look pretty in a natural way, without sleeping in curlers and putting that dreadful make-up on your face,' said Bonnie, staring hard at the girl. 'You've put that awful black stuff on your eyes again! Don't say that you haven't, for I can see it!'

'Well, I just put a little on,' admitted Esme sheepishly. 'I didn't think anyone would notice.'

Amy and Bonnie pursed their lips in disapproval and Amy said, 'Well, you must promise never to wear it again. And you must agree to do everything that we say.'

'Oh, I shall,' said Esme, nodding eagerly, feeling quite thrilled. She had made two friends, and she was going to please her mother by becoming more English. Perhaps things at Malory Towers weren't going to be so bad after all!

Julie and Lucy, meanwhile, were discussing their favourite subject – their horses.

'I can't wait until Saturday,' said Julie, her eyes shining. 'We can spend the whole day over at Five Oaks with Jack and Sandy.'

'I say, do you mind if Susan and I come along too?' asked Felicity, overhearing. 'I haven't seen Bill and Clarissa in simply ages.'

'The more the merrier!' said Julie, happily.

'In that case, I'll come as well,' said June. 'How about you, Freddie?'

Freddie nodded eagerly and Pam said, 'I say, why don't we all go and spend the day there? We could take a picnic along with us.'

'My word, what a super idea!' said Nora, clapping her hands together. Then she called out to Esme, Amy and Bonnie, 'I say, you three! We're all going to take a picnic to Five Oaks on Saturday. What about it?'

Amy, who was absolutely terrified of getting freckles if she spent too much time in the sun, shook her head and said, 'No, thank you. I don't want to ruin my complexion.'

'And I want to get on with the handkerchiefs I'm embroidering for Mother's birthday,' said Bonnie.

Esme hesitated. She wasn't afraid of going out in the sun, for her skin always turned an attractive golden brown. And she *so* wanted to see Sandy again! But she desperately wanted to keep in with Amy and Bonnie, and perhaps they wouldn't like it if she went off with the others. Amy solved her dilemma by murmuring in a low voice, 'Actually, it's a very good thing that they're all going out on Saturday. Bonnie and I can give you your first lesson in "Englishness", without *them* sticking their noses in and making fun of us.'

'Yes, we'll make an English rose of you yet, Esme!' said Bonnie.

'Gee, that's wunnerful!' cried Esme. 'I mean, gosh, how wizard!'

It was a happy group of third formers who went to bed that evening. Most of them were looking forward with great anticipation to their day out on Saturday, while Esme was delighted to have been accepted by Amy and Bonnie. Even Amy felt excited at the prospect of teaching Esme to become a lady, just like herself. She had never realised before just how much the girl looked up to her and wanted to be like her, and that kind of admiration was very pleasant to Amy. What a feather in her cap it would be if she could transform the American girl!

The following day, June had another encounter with Eleanor Banks. She, Freddie, Felicity and Susan were playing a game of doubles on the tennis-court. Amanda walked past with the Head Girl, Kay Foster, and, knowing that it was a free period for the third formers, she smiled and called out, 'My word, you girls are keen! That's just what I like to see. Keep it up, and I don't see how you can fail to get places on one of the teams!'

The four girls felt quite thrilled at Amanda's praise, and her words seemed to spur them on, all of them playing their hardest. Susan sent a particularly high ball across the net, placing it where June had no hope at all of returning it. But, being June, she had to try anyway, making a wild swipe at the ball and sending it soaring over the high mesh fence that surrounded the court. Unfortunately for June, Eleanor Banks happened to be walking by at that moment, and the ball bounced off the top of her head, causing her to squeal loudly.

'Gosh, sorry, Eleanor!' called out June.

But the fifth former was in no mood for apologies, although she had been more shocked than hurt, and she came over to the fence to scold June for her carelessness.

'It really was an accident, Eleanor,' said Felicity, hoping to placate the angry girl. But it was no use, for Eleanor disliked June intensely and was glad of any excuse to dish out a punishment. June, for her part, knew that it was useless to protest and kept her head down, hoping that if she put on a display of meekness, Eleanor would not give

41

her too many lines to learn. And that's when she noticed that one of Eleanor's shoelaces had come undone. At once all thoughts of pretending to be meek vanished from June's head and, giving Freddie a nudge, she whispered, 'Distract her.'

'What? How?' Freddie hissed back, looking rather alarmed.

'I don't know! Think of something – quickly!' muttered June.

So Freddie did the only thing she could think of, and pointed rather wildly in the direction of a large tree, which stood just outside the tennis-court, crying dramatically, 'Look!'

Everyone but June turned their heads at once, Felicity saying, 'What is it, Freddie?'

'Can't you see it?' said Freddie. 'My word, I've never seen anything like it in my life!'

'But what *is* it?' demanded Eleanor, growing impatient. 'I can't see anything at all!'

'Nor can I, Freddie,' said Susan. 'What is it? A bird, or a squirrel or something?'

'Yes, that's it – a squirrel!' said Freddie. 'But it was no ordinary squirrel, for it was absolutely enormous.'

June, meanwhile, grinning to herself, had worked swiftly. The wicked girl had crouched down and pulled both ends of Eleanor's shoelace through the holes in the mesh, knotting them together very tightly, several times.

June straightened up as Eleanor snapped, 'Enough of this nonsense! I don't believe that there's anything in the tree at all.' Then she turned her head to glare at June and felt in her pocket for the little punishment book that all the fifth- and sixth-form girls carried with them. With a triumphant little smirk she pulled it out, at the same time going to take a step back from the fence. And that was when she discovered that she was quite unable to move her foot, for June had tied it securely to the fence! Felicity, Susan and Freddie noticed her predicament at once, the three of them gasping at June's audacity and struggling to hide their laughter as Eleanor roared, 'June! Untie my shoelace at once!'

But June pretended not to hear, and called to the others, 'Come on, you three! Let's carry on with our game.'

Freddie was at her side at once, but the more responsible Felicity and Susan hesitated. As head-girl of the form, she really ought to release the fifth former, Felicity thought, watching as Eleanor bent down, pushing her fingers through the mesh, and struggling to untie the knots in her shoelace. She wasn't having much success, though, for June had done her work well and the knots were very tight indeed.

Felicity and Susan exchanged a doubtful look, then an enraged squeal from Eleanor made them both burst into laughter.

'Felicity Rivers!' yelled the infuriated girl, red in the face with anger and humiliation. 'How dare you laugh at me? I shall report you to Miss Potts, all four of you!'

'The chances are that she'll report us whether we help her or not,' said Felicity with a chuckle. 'So we may as well have some fun!'

And with that, she and Susan picked up their rackets and took their places on the court.

'I say, Eleanor,' June called out. 'Throw us our ball back, will you? Oh no, you can't – you're a little tied up!'

The others roared with laughter, as the furious Eleanor, angry tears starting to her eyes now, beat at the fence with her fists, and Susan said, 'Not to worry, June, I have a spare ball in my pocket. Your service, I think!'

As the girls played on, Eleanor continued to work at the knots in her shoelace, and at last she managed to undo two of them. She gave a little cry of triumph, and began tugging at the third and final one. But this knot proved even more difficult and, in frustration, Eleanor screamed, causing June to drawl, 'My goodness, I don't think I've ever seen the Ice Queen get so hot and bothered. Careful, Eleanor, or you'll melt!'

In sheer frustration, the laughter of the third formers ringing in her ears, Eleanor kicked out at the fence with her free foot, and it was at this moment that Amanda returned to the court, with a small group of fifth formers, all dressed for tennis, in tow.

'Hey!' shouted Amanda, angrily. 'Eleanor Banks! What on *earth* do you think you're playing at?'

Horrified to be caught in such an embarrassing situation by members of her own form, Eleanor bent down and gave the knot a last, violent tug, and it came loose so suddenly that she toppled over backwards. Eleanor was not popular with her own form, and the laughter of the fifth formers joined with that of the third formers now, as

Amanda marched across to her and said wrathfully, 'How dare you distract the youngsters from their tennis practice with your fooling around? At your age, Eleanor, you really should know better!'

'But I wasn't fooling around, Amanda!' the girl protested. 'It was that beast of a June! She tied me to the fence when I wasn't looking, and –'

'What nonsense!' said Amanda scornfully. 'When I walked by this court, a short while ago, June was working hard at her tennis and she is *still* playing tennis now. It's a pity that you didn't have half of her dedication, Eleanor, then you could focus your energy on something worthwhile instead of disrupting everyone else. As you're a fifth former, I can't punish you as you deserve, but you had better jolly well stay out of my way, let me tell you!'

Eleanor, realising that it was pointless to argue with Amanda in this mood, murmured something which might have been an apology and slunk away.

June, meanwhile, looking the picture of goodness, shook her head sorrowfully at the departing girl, before finishing her game of tennis under the approving eye of Amanda.

'And the best of it is that Eleanor didn't even get round to giving me a punishment,' laughed June carelessly as the four girls walked off the court afterwards.

'My goodness, I haven't laughed so much in ages!' said Freddie, still chuckling to herself.

'It was very funny,' agreed Felicity. 'But the Ice Queen is going to be out for revenge, June – so watch out!'

A visit to Five Oaks

Saturday dawned bright and sunny, and the third formers leapt out of bed eagerly – apart from Nora, who always hated leaving her comfortable bed, even on a glorious morning like this.

'Just five more minutes,' she mumbled drowsily, as Pam tried to rouse her.

'I know you, my girl,' said Pam sternly. 'Your five minutes will stretch into ten, then fifteen, and you'll end up being late for breakfast.'

'I know what will get her up,' said June, coming over and winking at Pam. 'A nice cold, wet sponge! I'll just go and fetch one, shall I?'

Had the speaker been anyone but June, Nora would have dismissed this as an idle threat. But there was no limit to June's daring, and one never knew what she would do next, so Nora sat up abruptly, a scowl on her face, and Pam swiftly grabbed the girl's arm, hauling her out of bed before she could lie down again.

The girls got themselves ready in record time and, after breakfast, went to the kitchen to collect the picnic baskets that the cook had promised to leave ready for them.

'She's done us proud,' said Felicity, lifting the lid of one of the baskets. 'There are sandwiches of every kind, sponge cake, fruit – ooh, and two big bottles of lemonade! It makes me feel hungry already, although I've just finished breakfast!'

The third formers were in high spirits as they made their way to Five Oaks, carrying the picnic baskets between them, and Felicity said, 'I don't know how Amy, Bonnie and Esme can bear to be cooped up indoors on such a beautiful day. It would do the three of them the world of good to get out in the fresh air and think about something else besides their looks.'

'Well, if that's their idea of fun, I suppose it's up to them,' said Susan. 'I say, I'm looking forward to seeing old Jack again, aren't you?'

Felicity nodded. 'Malory Towers just isn't the same without him, somehow, although he's not very far away.'

And Jack was very pleased to see the girls, too, being on the friendliest of terms with all of them. Everyone made a great fuss of him, feeding him sugar lumps and patting his velvety muzzle, and Lucy's horse, Sandy, in the next stall, became very jealous indeed, whinnying for his share of attention. The third formers could see how Sandy had got his name, for he was the most beautiful pale, golden-brown colour.

'Just like the sand on the beach,' as Nora said, stroking his broad neck. 'He's adorable, Lucy.'

Julie turned to the young stable lad, who was busily cleaning some tack, and asked, 'Where are Bill and Clarissa, Jim?'

'Up at the house, miss,' he answered, and Felicity said, 'Well, let's pop in and say hallo.'

The girls walked across the stable-yard to the pretty little house that Bill and Clarissa shared, and Pam pushed at the door. To her surprise, it didn't budge, and she said, 'That's odd! I've never known Bill and Clarissa to lock their door before. Normally we just walk straight in.'

She rapped sharply on the door and, after a few moments, it opened slightly and a pale, thin face with bright green eyes and a worried expression appeared at the crack. Then the worried expression cleared, replaced by a smile, and the door was pulled wide open.

'Girls!' exclaimed Clarissa Carter. 'How lovely to see you all. Do come in!'

She stood aside, and the third formers filed past her into the big, cosy kitchen, where a young woman with short, dark hair and a tanned complexion sat at a large wooden table, looking rather pensive.

'Bill!' cried Felicity. 'I do hope you don't mind us all turning up like this.'

'Of course not!' said Bill, her face creasing into a smile. 'It's wonderful to see you all. I say, you've brought a picnic too – how marvellous!'

'Put your baskets over in the corner there, girls,' said Clarissa. 'It's in the shade, so everything will stay nice and cool.'

The girls did so, then Bill said, 'I'm afraid you'll have to take it in turns if you all want to ride, for we only have four horses free today.'

'I'm happy just to watch the others,' said Felicity, who was fond of horses, but wasn't a great rider.

'The same goes for me,' said Nora. 'I'm just here for a day out and a picnic!'

'I say, Clarissa, why was the door locked?' asked Pam. 'It's normally open house here.'

Bill and Clarissa exchanged worried glances and Felicity asked, 'Is anything wrong?'

'Well, yes, actually,' said Clarissa, gravely. 'I'm afraid a couple of things have gone wrong just lately.'

The third formers looked alarmed, and Bill said, 'Clarissa and I were giving riding lessons to some of the children from the village a couple of days ago, and while we were in the paddock, someone simply walked into the house and stole our cash-box.'

The girls were very fond of Bill and Clarissa, and knew how hard they had worked to make a success of the riding stables, so there was an immediate outcry at this.

'That's simply dreadful!'

'I wish I could get my hands on whoever did it – mean beasts!'

'Was there much money in the box?'

'Did you call the police?'

'Luckily there wasn't an awful lot of money in the box,' said Clarissa. 'But the thought that someone just walked in and helped himself – or herself – is most worrying, as you can imagine. That's why we have started to get into the habit of locking the door.'

'And we called the police,' added Bill. 'But the thief

didn't leave any clues at all, so they weren't able to be of much help. There's something else, too.'

Bill looked very serious indeed, and the third formers looked at her anxiously. Then she went on, 'Last night, while we were in bed, someone let Merrylegs out – and they left the gate open too. We got the horse back, but if he had got on to the road it could have ended very badly indeed.'

The girls exchanged horrified glances. Merrylegs was Clarissa's own horse, and the girls knew how dearly she loved him.

'I wish he had gone for my Thunder instead,' said Bill grimly, her eyes glinting. 'He's not as friendly with strangers as Merrylegs, and would certainly have given the intruder a rough time!'

'Are you sure that someone let Merrylegs out deliberately?' asked Freddie. 'I mean – isn't it possible that one of you didn't lock the stable door properly?'

Clarissa shook her head. 'Bill and I always go round and check everything thoroughly before we go to bed. And everything was just as it should be last night. Besides, I saw someone in the yard.'

The third formers gasped and Clarissa continued, 'I was asleep, and something woke me – some sort of noise from outside. I got up and went to the window, and saw someone in the yard.'

'Did you recognise them?' asked Susan, her eyes wide.

'No,' said Clarissa, with a sigh. 'It was too dark, and this person was dressed from head to toe in black. In fact, it was impossible even to tell whether they were male or female. But whoever it was looked up and saw me standing at the bedroom window, then made a run for it.'

'How about you, Bill?' asked Nora. 'Did you see or hear anything?'

'No, for my bedroom is at the other side of the house,' answered Bill. 'Of course, Clarissa woke me immediately and we ran down into the yard – and that's when we discovered that Merrylegs had been let out.'

The third formers looked at one another. It was all very mysterious – and very worrying, especially for Julie and Lucy, who had horses of their own at Five Oaks. Clarissa looked at the grave faces of the two girls and said, 'If you want to remove Jack and Sandy, we will quite understand. There are a couple of other riding stables in the area, but they are a few miles away from Malory Towers.'

But Julie said loyally, 'I wouldn't dream of taking Jack away. I know that you and Bill will do all you can to keep him safe.'

'And Sandy is staying too,' said Lucy. 'I shall teach him to kick out at anyone who is a stranger to him.'

Clarissa and Bill smiled, and Pam, who had been looking thoughtful, said, 'Do you think that the person who let Merrylegs out intended to steal him?'

'I don't know,' said Clarissa, with a sigh. 'He's not a particularly valuable horse, though he's priceless to me, of course. I would have thought that any horse thief would have gone to Mr Banks's along the road, for he keeps racehorses, and some of them are worth a lot of money.'

'That's a thought!' exclaimed Bill. 'I wonder if Mr Banks has had any unwanted night-time visitors at his stable-yard? I must remember to ask Eleanor when she pops over to ride Snowball later.'

'Is Eleanor keeping Snowball here?' asked June, looking puzzled. 'That seems odd, when her uncle has a perfectly good stable just a short distance away.'

'Yes, but it's full,' explained Clarissa. 'Mr Banks has bought several more horses recently, so there wasn't room for Eleanor to keep Snowball there. She usually visits him on Saturday mornings, so if there has been any funny business going on over there, Eleanor is sure to know. Anyway, I'm quite sure that you girls didn't come along here to listen to our woes, and we certainly don't want to spoil your day. Now, off you go outside and enjoy yourselves!'

And the third formers did just that! Julie and Lucy cantered round the big paddock on Jack and Sandy, with June and Freddie in hot pursuit on two of the riding-school ponies. Pam and Susan followed more sedately, while Felicity and Nora had a simply marvellous time watching the others, helping Jim with his chores and enjoying the sunshine. But as they ate their picnic in the paddock, the subject of Bill and Clarissa's troubles came to the fore again.

'It's strange that they should have had two strokes of bad luck in a matter of a few days,' mused Felicity, tucking into a sandwich.

'Very strange,' said June. 'In fact, it's almost as if

someone was out to cause trouble for them.'

'Surely not!' cried Susan, looking shocked. 'Why, dear old Bill and Clarissa don't have an enemy in the world!'

'Of course they don't!' said Julie. 'Everyone likes them.'

'Don't bite my head off!' said June. 'But it's quite clear that someone *doesn't* like them – the person who stole their money. And the person who let Merrylegs out. I wonder if they are one and the same?'

There was a brief silence as the third formers digested this, and at last Pam said, 'Well, at least Bill and Clarissa have been put on their guard now. If the troublemaker comes back and tries anything else, he might not find it so easy.'

When the girls had finished eating, and cleared away the remains of their picnic, they went into the stable-yard to find Bill talking to Eleanor Banks, who was mounted on a most beautiful pure white horse, with a snowy mane and tail, and the watching third formers stared.

'My word, what a super horse!' said Susan.

'He's certainly perfect for the Ice Queen,' said Felicity wryly.

'He's a great deal too good for her, if you ask me,' said Julie, with a frown. 'I don't believe that Eleanor cares for Snowball at all. She seems to see him as a possession, and doesn't love him as I love Jack, or as Lucy loves Sandy.'

Eleanor certainly cut an elegant figure in her smart riding gear, sitting up very straight in the saddle as she rode Snowball into the paddock. She gave June a cold glare as she passed the third formers, and the girl gave an exaggerated shiver. 'Brr, it suddenly seems to have turned chilly round here. Eleanor is so cold that I simply can't imagine her caring for anyone or anything!'

'I say, Bill!' called out Pam. 'Did you ask Eleanor if there had been any strange goings-on over at her uncle's stables?'

'Yes,' said Bill, coming over. 'But all has been quiet over there. She's going to warn Mr Banks to look out for anything suspicious, though.'

'Good,' said Julie. 'And now I suppose we had better get the horses back into the stables and make our way back to school.'

'I wonder what Amy, Bonnie and Esme have been doing while we've been enjoying our day at Five Oaks?' said Felicity, as the girls walked back to Malory Towers.

'Nothing very strenuous, I don't suppose,' said Susan with a grin. 'I bet they have been having a really lazy time of it!'

But in fact the three girls had, in their own way, been very busy indeed. First of all, Bonnie had insisted that Esme throw away every scrap of make-up, and had actually stood over her while she did it.

'Gee, this seems such a waste!' Esme had complained, reluctantly removing everything from her bedside cabinet and putting it into the bin. 'Can't I just keep *one* lipstick?'

'Absolutely not!' said Bonnie firmly. 'And don't say "gee"!'

Then, to Esme's horror, Amy had brushed out her carefully set curls, saying, 'I'm sure that you will sleep much better at night without those curlers in your hair.'

'I expect that I will,' said Esme rather doubtfully. 'Ow! Don't brush so hard, Amy – that hurt!'

'Well, sit still, then,' said Amy, unsympathetically. 'There, that looks much better! And when you've got into the habit of brushing it one hundred times every night it will soon start to shine, just as mine does.'

'I sure hope so,' said Esme, staring at herself rather glumly in the mirror. 'At the moment it just looks kinda strange.'

'Kind of, not "kinda",' said Bonnie, clicking her tongue. 'And it just looks strange because you're not used to it yet.' Then she looked down at Esme's hands and gave a little squeal. 'Take that nail polish off at once! If Miss Peters sees you wearing it she'll have a fit.'

'But it took me simply ages to paint them,' moaned Esme. 'Do I have to take it off?'

'Yes,' said the two girls, in unison, eyeing her severely, and, sighing heavily, Esme obeyed.

'Now you're really beginning to look like an English schoolgirl,' said Bonnie happily. 'Isn't she, Amy?'

Amy, looking Esme over critically, nodded and said, 'But we really need to set to work on your speech. Now, repeat after me – *wonderful*.'

'Wunnerful,' said Esme.

'Won*d*erful!' said Bonnie. 'It has a d in the middle, you know!'

Esme took a deep breath, a very determined look on her face, and said, 'Wunnerful.'

Amy and Bonnie shook their heads in despair, and Amy said, 'Oh dear. Perhaps you should just avoid saying wonderful altogether. Try "super" or "wizard" instead.'

But this wasn't good enough for Bonnie, who said firmly, 'No, that's just avoiding the problem, instead of solving it. Esme, try saying twenty.'

'Twenny,' said Esme, obligingly.

Bonnie frowned. 'Hmm. I don't know why you should find it difficult to pronounce words with t or d in the middle, but it's quite obvious that you do. Well, we can't do much about it now, for the others will be back soon, but I shall think of a way to overcome your problem.'

'Do you think you can?' said Esme, hopefully. 'If you could, it would be just wunner– I mean, just super!'

6

Secrets and surprises

Of course, it wasn't easy to keep a secret in the third form, and the girls soon found out that Amy and Bonnie were taking Esme 'in hand', as they called it. Everyone approved wholeheartedly of the change in Esme's appearance, and thought that she looked very nice indeed. And they were much amused by her attempts to imitate Amy's high, well-bred voice. It really did sound very funny, especially when the girl used English phrases that she had picked up from the others, then suddenly lapsed back into her American drawl.

'I say,' she said to June – in what the girls had come to call her 'Amy voice' – over breakfast one morning. 'Would you pass me the salt, old girl?'

June, her eyes narrowing with amusement, had passed her the salt cellar, and Esme went on, 'My word, these scrambled eggs are simply top-hole. Yessir, they sure are mighty fine.'

Then she looked completely bewildered when the girls burst into laughter, for poor Esme didn't seem to realise that she was switching from one way of speaking to the other.

'She's absolutely priceless,' chuckled Felicity, as she and Susan discussed it later that day.

'Well, they do say that imitation is the sincerest form of flattery,' said Susan, with a grin. 'But Amy didn't seem awfully flattered by Esme's attempt to mimic her accent!'

'I hope that she doesn't try to copy Amy and Bonnie *too* slavishly,' said Felicity, wrinkling her brow. 'That would be an awful shame!'

'Yes,' said Susan, thoughtfully. 'I know that none of us is perfect, but the two of them have more faults than most. Amy especially! It would have been much better if Esme had decided to model herself on someone down-to-earth and friendly and jolly, like you, or Pam, or Julie.'

'I think it would be best if Esme didn't copy anyone at all,' said Felicity thoughtfully. 'Her own personality is very pleasant and unique, and it would be a terrible pity if she lost her individuality through trying too hard to be something that she isn't.'

'You're quite right, of course, old girl,' said Susan. 'It must be awfully difficult for Esme, though, for I know that she wants to please her mother by learning English ways.'

'I expect that she will, after she's been here for a while,' said Felicity. 'But she must learn them in her own time and in her own way. It's no use trying to force things like that.'

But Bonnie, who could be extremely stubborn once she got an idea into her head, was determined that she was going to teach Esme to pronounce 'wonderful' correctly if it was the last thing she did! She spent ages coaching Esme, who soon grew heartily bored and began to wish that she hadn't asked the two girls for their help.

'Can't we do something else instead?' she complained, after failing in her pronunciation for about the tenth time. 'I'll never be able to say wonderful properly, so I might as well give up!'

Bonnie stared at the girl, hardly able to believe her ears. 'But you *did* say it!' she cried. 'You just said it then – wonderful!'

'Gee, did I?' asked Esme, looking stunned. 'Why, that's – wonderful!'

A delighted Bonnie clapped her hands together and squealed, 'Well done, Esme! Oh, how I wish that the others were here to listen to you.'

But the two of them were alone in the common-room. Amy had been called to Matron's room over the matter of some badly darned stockings, while the rest of the third form were outside enjoying the sunshine. Just then, Lucy came in to fetch her plimsolls from her locker, and Bonnie cried, 'I say, Lucy, isn't it marvellous? Your cousin has learned to say wonderful properly.'

'What an achievement,' sneered Lucy, looking at Esme with contempt. 'Honestly, Esme, I'm not surprised that Miss Grayling put you into the third form instead of the fourth. In fact, it's a wonder she didn't put you in with the first-form babies! But perhaps even they would have been too advanced for you, for they know how to speak English properly. As for you, Bonnie, I don't know how you can be bothered to waste your time on Esme – I really don't!'

And, before her cousin could retaliate, she snatched up her plimsolls and stalked out of the room, leaving Esme and Bonnie staring after her open-mouthed.

'Well!' exclaimed Bonnie, at last. 'How dreadfully rude of her.'

Esme shrugged, and managed a rueful smile as she said, 'That's Lucy for you. She never misses an opportunity to get in a dig at me.'

'But why?' asked Bonnie, frowning. 'It's none of my business, and I certainly don't mean to pry, but I just can't understand why she is so hostile towards you.'

Esme hesitated, then said, 'Well, it's all because of the family feud.'

'Family feud?' repeated Bonnie, her eyes wide.

Esme nodded solemnly, and began, 'This coldness between Lucy and me all started a few years ago. You see, our fathers became very good friends when they married sisters – my mother and Lucy's mother, of course. In fact the two of them used to joke that they were as close as brothers.' Esme sighed. 'It was such a good, happy life back in those days. We even lived next door to one another! Lucy and I were best friends then, too, and we were all just one big happy family.'

'So what went wrong?' asked Bonnie, astonished and quite unable to picture the two cousins as best friends.

'Well, Uncle Robert – Lucy's father – and my father are both interested in antiques,' said Esme. 'So they decided to buy a shop and run it together. It seemed like a splendid idea at the time, but that's when things started to go wrong. You see, my father and Uncle Robert are both very strong personalities, and each of them had quite different ideas about the way the shop should be run. Both of them wanted to take charge, and they began to argue quite dreadfully, for neither of them would consider the other's point of view, or agree to any kind of compromise.'

'Goodness!' said Bonnie, her eyes like saucers. 'That must have put a terrible strain on their friendship.'

'It did,' said Esme. 'For it was quite impossible for them to switch off their feelings of anger once they had finished work for the day. Soon Father and Uncle Robert were barely on speaking terms with one another. Of course, it started to affect our mothers, for mine felt that she had to take Father's side, while Aunt Janet took Uncle Robert's. It was horrible for them, because twins are so close and they had spent their whole lives together. I know that my mother was awfully upset about it, and I'm quite sure that Aunt Janet felt the same. To be fair, though, they did try to keep Lucy and me out of it, and never tried to stop the two of us from seeing one another. But we couldn't help overhearing things, and we soon figured out what was going on. And then, one day, we quarrelled as well. Lucy was trying to blame my father for things going wrong, and made some very hurtful remarks about him. Of course, I stuck up for him and said some pretty awful things about Uncle Robert.'

Esme shuddered at the memory and said, 'It was a dreadful row. Really horrible and vicious! Lucy said that she would never forgive me, but the things that she said about my father were just as cruel and nasty.'

'So your friendship with Lucy was spoiled too,' said

Bonnie, looking very grave. 'It just goes to show how family rows can get out of hand.'

'Well, this one certainly did,' said Esme, sighing. 'The next thing that happened was that Father announced that he couldn't work with Uncle Robert any longer. He told Mother and I that the shop was going up for sale, and that we were moving to America.'

'Heavens!' said Bonnie. 'That must have been a shock.'

'It was,' said Esme sadly. 'Mother didn't want to go, and nor did I, at first. We both hoped that Father and Uncle Robert might make up, but they never did. The shop was sold, and off we went.'

It was quite a sad story, thought Bonnie, and neither Esme's father, nor Lucy's, came out of it particularly well. Bonnie felt a sudden wave of anger. The two men had sacrificed the happiness of their wives and daughters, and split their big, happy family right down the middle. And all because they were both too stubborn to swallow their silly pride!

Suddenly the door of the common-room burst open and Amy stalked in, an angry scowl on her face. She was carrying a pile of stockings and she flung them down crossly, before flopping down in an armchair.

'Matron is a mean beast!' she declared. 'She's told me that I have to darn all these stockings again, because I haven't done them properly.'

'Well, I must say, Amy, she's quite right!' said Bonnie, picking up one of the stockings and examining it critically. 'I simply can't believe that someone who prides herself on her appearance, as you do, would use bright red wool for darning.'

'It was all I could find,' said Amy impatiently. 'Besides, I don't see why I should have to darn them at all. Why can't I just go out and buy new ones? It's not as if I can't afford them!'

'Because the rule is, that if you tear your things, you have to mend them,' said Bonnie, imitating Matron's crisp tone. 'I say, Amy, I don't mind darning these for you, if you do my French prep for me. What do you say?'

Amy looked thoughtful. This was a little arrangement that had worked well for the two girls until last term. Bonnie had done all of Amy's mending for her, while Amy had returned the favour by doing Bonnie's French prep. But Felicity had got wise to this scheme after a while, and put a stop to it.

'Bonnie, it's out and out cheating for Amy to do your French for you,' she had told the girl roundly. 'And as for you, Amy, I know you don't like mending. Nor do I, come to that! But, sadly, we all have to learn to do things that we don't like at times.'

Amy considered Bonnie's offer for a moment now, and reluctantly shook her head, saying, 'We shall only get into a beastly row from Felicity.'

'Ah, but Felicity isn't here,' pointed out Bonnie.

'No, but she could come back at any time,' said Amy, who was a little more in awe of Felicity than she cared to admit. The head-girl had a way of speaking to wrong-doers that made them feel very small indeed, and

Amy was in no mood for a scolding today.

'I suppose I shall just have to do it myself,' she sighed. 'You and Esme can chat to me whilst I work.'

But Esme had just glanced at her watch, and now she jumped to her feet, saying, 'Sorry, Amy, I must dash. It's almost time for my tennis practice and Amanda will be livid if I'm late.'

'It's a pity that you didn't come to me for advice before you let yourself in for all this extra coaching,' said Bonnie. 'I could have got you out of it.'

Esme, who was extremely impressed by Bonnie's talent for getting out of anything that she didn't wish to do, asked curiously, 'How come Amanda never picks on you, Bonnie?'

'Because she thinks that I try hard,' answered Bonnie. 'Whenever I see Amanda coming, I run and jump around the court for all I'm worth. But somehow I still never manage to hit a ball. So she's under the impression that – although I'm completely hopeless – it's the best I can do. And Amanda never wastes her time on anyone who she thinks is hopeless. Now, someone who has ability, but doesn't try, is a completely different matter!'

Amused, Esme laughed and said ruefully, 'If only I had known that earlier! But Amanda has got it into her head that she's going to make a good player out of me.'

Amanda had stuck to her word and was keeping Esme's nose to the grindstone as far as tennis was concerned. And, somewhat to her own surprise, the girl's game had improved dramatically.

As Esme walked down to meet Amanda, she could see Felicity and Susan having a fast and furious game on one of the courts, while on another, June was playing against Vanessa Tyler, a big East Tower girl. Esme couldn't help whistling softly to herself in admiration as June leapt high in the air to return Vanessa's serve, sending the ball whizzing past the bigger girl. Gee, thought Esme to herself, I wonder if I'll ever be half as good as that? Then she suddenly stopped in her tracks, horrified. Surely she wasn't turning into one of these jolly, sporting types of girl? Why, the thought was just too horrible to contemplate. Whatever would Amy and Bonnie say?

Amanda had spotted Esme and called out sharply, 'Come along, Esme! Don't dawdle. You're playing against Freddie today, and I want to see both of you doing your very best.'

But what Esme, Freddie and the others didn't realise was that Amanda was going to be watching them very closely indeed. For she had just arranged a very important tournament against a nearby school, and today the games captain was going to be making some decisions that could affect the outcome.

Freddie was a good player, but she had several weaknesses and Esme soon spotted these and learned how to turn them to her advantage. Esme, who hadn't been looking forward to the practice at all, soon lost herself in the game, and felt a peculiar thrill of pride when – to the astonishment of everyone watching – she narrowly beat her opponent.

'Jolly well played, Esme!' yelled Amanda, coming on to the court to clap the girl on the back, which she did so vigorously that Esme almost lost her balance!

Felicity also beat Susan, while June, in a very close-fought match indeed, triumphed over Vanessa. Amanda gathered all the players around her and said in her loud voice, 'I'm very pleased with all of you. You have all proved today that you are made of good stuff. Now, I want you to listen carefully. In a few weeks time, I will be taking a team of players to St Margaret's school, to compete against them in a tennis tournament. June and Vanessa, I want you both to represent Malory Towers in the lower-school singles matches. Felicity and Susan, you two will be taking part in the doubles.'

The four girls looked at one another, their eyes shining in wonder and delight. Hurrah! They had been picked for the team! Even June, whose manner was normally very offhand, and who rarely got excited about anything, couldn't keep the broad grin off her face. My word, she would play up all right! Amanda wouldn't regret her decision, June would make sure of that. Then the games captain was speaking again.

'Esme,' she said. 'You are to be a reserve, so if any of the four girls are unable to play on the day, you may have to take their place.'

'*Me?*' squeaked Esme, hardly able to believe her ears. 'Amanda, are you quite sure that you don't mean Freddie?'

'I'm quite sure,' said Amanda, laughing at the girl's expression of disbelief. 'You've worked very hard at your tennis, Esme, and come on in leaps and bounds. And this is your reward. Now, I want you to keep up your practice, and make sure that you get to know how Felicity and Susan play, for if one of them has to drop out you may have to partner the other.'

Esme listened to all this with her head in a whirl, and very mixed feelings. What *had* she let herself in for? Yes, she had worked hard at her tennis, but only to avoid getting into a row with Amanda. She had never even *thought* of getting on to the team.

Felicity guessed at her thoughts and, as they made their way back to school, clapped her on the shoulder and said, 'Don't look so worried, old girl. You're only reserve, after all, and the chances are you won't even have to play. I have no intention of getting ill, or breaking my leg, or anything silly like that. And nor has Susan.'

'And I shall be there all right, too,' said June, a determined look on her face. 'Come on, everyone, let's find the others and tell them the news. I say, where are Pam and Nora?'

The third formers couldn't find Pam and Nora, but they did spot Julie and Lucy, who had just returned from a ride at Five Oaks and were walking across the courtyard.

Susan hailed them, calling out, 'Hi, you two! My word, you'll never guess what has happened!'

'June, Susan and I have been picked for the tennis team!' yelled Felicity, rushing up to them. 'And Esme is reserve!'

Then she stopped, for Julie and Lucy didn't seem to be

listening to what she was saying at all. And now that she looked at them properly, the expressions on their faces were unusually grave. Heavens, *whatever* could have happened?

The third form rallies round

The others had noticed that the two girls looked unusually serious too, and glanced at one another apprehensively, as Felicity asked in alarm, 'I say, what's up? Don't tell me there has been more trouble over at Five Oaks?'

'I'm afraid that there has,' said Julie, her open, freckled face looking troubled. 'Someone has been hurt.'

'No!' gasped Susan. 'Who?'

'Let's go and sit under that tree,' said Julie, as a noisy group of first formers began playing with a ball nearby. 'And we'll tell you all about it.'

So the third formers sat in the shade of a large apple tree and Lucy said, 'Bill was riding Thunder, and showing a group of children how to take one of the practice jumps, when she fell off. We don't know how badly hurt she is yet, but it looks as if she's injured her arm.'

'*Bill?*' repeated June, incredulously. 'But Bill is a superb horsewoman! How could she possibly have had an accident taking one of those titchy little jumps?'

'That's just it,' said Julie, lowering her voice. 'It was no accident!'

'Whatever do you mean?' asked Freddie, looking puzzled.

'Well,' began Julie, 'when Bill fell off, everyone ran

across to help her, of course. Miss Peters was there – she's great friends with Bill and Clarissa, you know – and she said it looked as if the reins had snapped. But a little later, once all the fuss had died down, Lucy and I took a look at the reins, and it was quite clear that the reins hadn't snapped – they had been cut.'

'That's right,' said Lucy. 'It was a clean, straight cut, and there was no sign of wear, or fraying, as there would have been if they had simply snapped. Whoever did it only cut part of the way through, so that Bill wouldn't notice it immediately.'

'But why didn't Miss Peters notice that they had been cut?' asked Freddie, looking puzzled.

'She was more concerned with Bill than anything else,' said Julie. 'And she only glanced quickly at the reins.'

'So where is Bill now?' asked Felicity.

'At the hospital,' answered Lucy. 'Mr Banks took her there in his car and Miss Peters went with them.'

'Mr Banks? What on earth was he doing there?' asked Susan, astonished.

'Oh, he wasn't there, but Eleanor was,' said Julie. 'She saw at once that we needed someone with a car to take Bill to hospital, so she telephoned him from Five Oaks and he was there in a trice. I must say that he's quite different from what I expected.'

'Yes, he seemed awfully nice,' put in Lucy. 'And he was so concerned about Bill. He said that he would wait at the hospital for her and Miss Peters, and bring them both home again.'

'Quite different from Eleanor, then,' said June dryly. 'I say, Julie, who else was over at Five Oaks?'

Julie wrinkled her brow thoughtfully and said, 'A few youngsters from the village – oh, and Patsy and Rose from the second form. They have just started taking riding lessons. Then, of course, there was Jim, the stable boy.'

'Well, I can't imagine that any of *them* would have cut through Bill's reins!' said Felicity. 'We can certainly rule Miss Peters out. Patsy and Rose are fond of the odd joke, but they're good-hearted kids and wouldn't do anything so dangerous.'

'And it can't have been one of the village children, for they are hardly more than babies,' said Julie.

'What about Jim?' said Lucy, suddenly. 'I know that Bill and Clarissa are fond of him, but . . .'

Her voice tailed off as the others shook their heads, Felicity saying firmly, 'Jim has been working at Five Oaks since the girls opened the riding stables. It's quite unthinkable that he could have done such a thing.'

'That leaves Julie, Lucy and Eleanor who could have carried out the dark deed, then,' said June smoothly.

'I can assure you that Lucy and I are innocent,' said Julie stiffly, turning an angry red and glaring at June.

'Ass!' laughed June, giving her a push. 'Of course I know that you and Lucy are innocent! But I'm not so certain about Eleanor.'

'Surely she couldn't be responsible!' said Susan. 'I know that you don't like her, June – well, to be honest, none of us cares for her very much – but she always seems to have got along with Bill and Clarissa all right.'

'Yes, and soon as Bill fell she ran to telephone her uncle for help,' Lucy pointed out.

'Besides, it might not be anyone who was there today,' said Felicity, who had been thinking. 'Someone could have sneaked into the stables overnight and cut Thunder's reins then.'

'That's true,' said Julie. 'My goodness, I wish we could find out who was behind this beastly campaign! Wouldn't I like to tell them what I think of them!'

Miss Peters took the third formers for prep that evening, and her expression was unusually grim, thought Felicity, as if she was thinking very unpleasant thoughts. She seemed rather distracted too, and didn't even notice when June and Freddie whispered and giggled together, a crime that would normally have earned them a very severe punishment!

Felicity, Susan, Julie and Lucy stayed behind when prep was over, and went up to the mistress's desk.

'Miss Peters?' began Julie, rather hesitantly. 'We wondered if there was any news of Bill? Do you know how she is?'

Miss Peters looked into the anxious faces of the four girls, and her own stern expression relaxed a little, as she thought what kind, thoughtful girls they were.

'I'm afraid that Bill has broken her arm,' said Miss Peters. 'Fortunately it was a clean break, but it will be in plaster for a while, and it means that she won't be able to ride or be of much help in the stables for the next few weeks.'

The girls were very dismayed at this. Poor old Bill! And poor Clarissa. She and Jim were going to find it very hard work running the stables between the two of them, without Bill's assistance.

A thought occurred to Felicity and she said, 'Perhaps some of us could help! We could go over to Five Oaks before tea, or when we have a free period, and see if there's anything we can do.'

'That's a very kind idea, Felicity,' said Miss Peters, smiling. 'And I'm sure that Bill and Clarissa would appreciate it. Just as long as you don't let it interfere with your school work.'

The eager third formers assured Miss Peters that they wouldn't, then Julie said, rather seriously, 'Miss Peters, I think that there's something I ought to tell you. You see, after you and Bill went to the hospital with Mr Banks, Lucy and I had a look at those reins and –'

'I know, Julie,' Miss Peters broke in. 'They had been cut. I spotted it immediately.'

'Did you?' said Julie, surprised. 'But you didn't say anything at the time.'

'Well, I thought that there was quite enough drama going on,' said the mistress. 'And the immediate need was to get poor Bill to a hospital. However, I have informed Clarissa of my suspicions, though I've advised her to keep it from Bill for a few days. She will only fret over it, and that might hinder her recovery, you know.'

'Yes, of course,' said Felicity, a deep frown on her face. 'What with this and the other things that have happened,

73

it really does look as if someone is out to make trouble for Bill and Clarissa. I just wish we knew why!'

'So you know about the other incidents?' said Miss Peters, looking sharply at Felicity, who nodded. 'Well, please don't spread it around the school,' said the mistress. 'It could be bad for the girls' business, and they have quite enough problems to deal with at the moment!'

The third formers nodded and Susan asked, 'Do you have any idea of who the troublemaker could be, Miss Peters?'

Miss Peters shook her head and said with a sigh, 'I only wish that I did, Susan! But I've wracked my brains and simply can't think of anyone who has a grudge against Bill and Clarissa.'

The third formers went to the common-room, to tell Pam and Nora – who hadn't heard about Bill's accident – the latest news. They were both very shocked, of course, and Nora said, 'I think it's a very good idea of yours, Felicity, for all of us to see if we can help out at Five Oaks. I certainly don't mind doing my bit.'

'You can count me in, as well,' said Pam.

Esme, who was sitting nearby with Amy and Bonnie, looked up, and wondered if she should volunteer as well. She didn't know this Bill and Clarissa that the girls were always talking about, and she certainly didn't relish the idea of getting her carefully manicured hands dirty, but it sure sounded like the two of them could do with all the help that they could get! Would Amy and Bonnie offer their services, she wondered, glancing at Amy. The girl was poring over a fashion magazine and didn't seem to have heard a word the others had said. No, helping out at the stables would be too much like hard work for Amy! Bonnie had also taken no part in the conversation, but she had been listening intently, and said now, 'Surely the most useful thing you can do for Bill and Clarissa is to catch the troublemaker.'

'Brilliant!' said June sarcastically. 'Why didn't we think of that? And just how do you suggest we go about it, Bonnie?'

'You set a trap,' replied Bonnie simply.

June opened her mouth to make a scathing retort, then shut it again abruptly. Actually, that wasn't a bad idea. In fact, it was a jolly good idea! The other third formers obviously thought so too, for they were looking at one another excitedly, and Nora said, 'Bonnie, you never cease to amaze me!'

Bonnie smiled, while Felicity said thoughtfully, 'We must plan it really carefully, if it's to work. Come on, girls, let's put our thinking caps on.'

There was silence in the common-room for a while, as the girls thought hard, but it seemed that it was all in vain. Even the ingenious June had to admit defeat, something she didn't like at all.

'I can't come up with a single idea,' she said, frowning.

'Nor can I,' sighed Pam. 'Perhaps we should sleep on it, and tomorrow we can get to work on it when our minds are fresh.'

'Good idea,' said Felicity. 'A few of us should pop over

to Five Oaks after tea as well, to see how Bill is, and offer our help. As long as we are back in time for prep it will be all right.'

'I shall come with you!' announced Bonnie rather grandly.

The third formers looked at one another in surprise. Felicity, amused at the way Bonnie sounded as if she was bestowing some great honour on them all, grinned, and even Amy looked up from her magazine, startled.

'Don't tell me that you're going to muck out a stable or groom a horse!' she said, wrinkling her nose in distaste.

'Of course not,' said Bonnie. 'But I'd like to have a look at the place. It might give me some ideas on how to set this trap of ours.'

'Well, goodness knows we could do with some!' said Susan. 'We'd better not all go, or we'll be tripping over one another. I think four of us should be enough.'

'All right,' said Felicity. 'So that's you, me, Bonnie – and who would like to be the fourth?'

'Me,' said June promptly, a very determined look on her face. June liked to be at the forefront of everything that went on in the third form. Not only that, but she prided herself on her ingenuity, and if anyone was going to come up with an idea to trap Bill and Clarissa's mystery troublemaker it was going to be her, and not Bonnie!

Esme, who felt that it was all right for her to volunteer her services if Bonnie was going, had been about to say that she would like to go, before June jumped in, and looked rather disgruntled. But she was mollified when Amy laid a hand on her arm and said, 'Thank goodness I shall have you here to keep me company tomorrow evening, Esme. I must say, I'm surprised at Bonnie choosing to spend her valuable free time in a smelly stable!'

A marvellous trick

There was a letter waiting for Lucy when she went down to breakfast the following morning. The girl read it as she ate, her expression growing rather serious, and Julie noticed that she seemed quiet afterwards.

'Anything wrong, old girl?' Julie asked her, when they went outside at break-time. 'I hope you haven't had bad news from home.'

'Oh no, nothing like that,' Lucy replied. 'The letter was from Mother, but it wasn't bad news. You see, I wrote to her at the end of my first week, and mentioned that Esme was at Malory Towers too. I thought that she would be quite as shocked as I was.'

'But she wasn't?' said Julie.

'No. Mother wrote that she hopes that Esme and I can be friends again, and that we won't let what has happened in the past spoil things,' said Lucy, looking troubled. 'I was most surprised to learn that she felt like that. And, to be honest, Julie, I don't know if it's possible for Esme and I *ever* to be friends again.'

'Lucy, what *did* happen in the past?' asked Julie, frowning. 'You can tell me to mind my own business if you want to, but sometimes it helps to confide in someone.'

Lucy looked at her friend's open, honest face and decided that perhaps it *would* help to tell someone the truth about why she and Esme were enemies. So, just as Esme had confided in Bonnie, Lucy poured out the whole story to Julie.

'Well,' said Julie, when the girl had finished, 'I can quite see why you and Esme find it difficult to be friends. But, really, what happened was nothing to do with either of you.'

'I suppose that's true,' sighed Lucy. 'But she's changed so much since living in America that I don't even know if the two of us have anything in common any more.'

'She's still the same Esme underneath,' said Julie wisely, taking her friend's arm. 'I think it would be a jolly good thing if you could make it up. But just don't go getting *too* friendly with her, that's all, or I shall be left out in the cold!'

'No chance of that!' laughed Lucy. 'Well, I can't see Esme and I becoming friends again overnight, but I shall try and be a little more civil to her.'

Immediately after tea, Felicity, Susan, June and Bonnie went over to Five Oaks. Bill was seated in a large, comfy armchair in the living-room, her feet up on a stool and a cup of tea at her elbow.

'Clarissa is taking very good care of me,' she told her visitors. 'And everyone has been very kind. So many people have called to see me, and Mr and Mrs Banks brought me that huge bouquet of flowers. Isn't it beautiful?'

It was indeed a beautiful bouquet, and so large that Clarissa had needed three vases to hold all the flowers.

'Mr Banks is awfully nice,' said Clarissa. 'Do you know, he even offered to lend us one of his stable boys for a few days to help out, but of course we wouldn't hear of it.'

'Goodness, that was kind of him!' said Felicity. 'But there's no need for you to worry about being short of help, because that's why we're here. A few of us third formers are going to come over and do what we can every day until Bill's arm is healed.'

The two girls thanked them heartily, and, after they had chatted to Bill for a little while, Clarissa took the third formers outside and set them to work.

Felicity and Susan helped Jim to muck out the stables, while June swept the yard. Bonnie, meanwhile, entertained everyone with her efforts to play detective.

'June!' she shrieked. 'There are hoof-prints over here by the gate! The intruder must have come on horseback.'

'My dear Bonnie,' sighed June. 'This is a riding stable. There are hoof-prints as far as the eye can see!'

'Oh, yes. I suppose there would be,' said Bonnie, rather crestfallen. But her spirits rose a little later when she discovered a scrap of green wool caught on one of the fences.

'Aha!' she cried. 'This could be a clue.'

Alas for Bonnie, her hopes were dashed again when Clarissa said, 'That's where I tore my green sweater the other day.'

Then, to the amusement of Felicity and Susan, Bonnie

subjected poor Jim to an intense grilling, before announcing her intention of going indoors to question Bill.

'No!' cried Felicity and Susan together.

'Bonnie, don't forget that Bill doesn't know yet that someone deliberately tried to harm her,' said Susan. 'And she doesn't need any more shocks at the moment.'

'Now what am I to do?' sighed Bonnie. 'I've explored every avenue, left no stone unturned . . .'

'You could always give us a hand,' suggested Felicity, without much hope.

But Bonnie suddenly decided that she had better look round the yard again, just in case there was anything she had missed!

June, her sharp eyes peeled for anything unusual, didn't fare any better. The one good thing about a routine chore like sweeping, she decided, was that it didn't need brains and gave one plenty of time to think. But all her thinking got her nowhere, and she was still unable to think up a scheme for trapping the mean beast who was making life so difficult for Bill and Clarissa.

'Well, that was a waste of time,' she said, rather glumly, on the way back to school.

'Nonsense,' said Felicity. 'We were able to be of help to the girls, so I don't think it was a waste of time at all.'

'But we're no nearer finding out who the culprit is,' said Bonnie.

'Cheer up!' said Susan, giving her a clap on the shoulder. 'One of us is bound to come up with an idea to trap him sooner or later.'

'Let's just hope it's sooner,' said June, impatiently.

An air of gloom seemed to hang over her and Bonnie after that, and when they got back to Malory Towers it seemed to pervade the whole form. In the common-room, after prep, everyone was rather quiet and listless and at last it all got too much for Freddie.

'For heaven's sake, cheer up!' she cried. 'I know it's disappointing that we're no nearer solving Bill and Clarissa's problems, but there's still plenty to celebrate. June, Felicity and Susan have all been picked for the tennis team, and Esme –'

She stopped suddenly, for Esme gave a cough and caught Freddie's eye. Freddie read the message she was conveying at once – Esme hadn't yet told Amy and Bonnie that she was to be reserve because she wasn't sure if they would approve! So Freddie went on smoothly, 'And Esme is becoming a proper English girl, thanks to Amy and Bonnie. I think that we should try to forget all of the bad things that are happening for a little while and plan some fun – a trick!'

This lifted everyone's spirits at once, and an excited murmur ran round the room.

'A trick! Marvellous!'

'What a super idea. Just what we need to take our minds off things.'

'June and Freddie's tricks are always so hilarious! I say, I wonder if they'll play it on Mam'zelle Dupont?'

'All right,' said June, a grin replacing her frown. 'I've got some things in the dorm that I ordered from one of my trick booklets. If we go up a few minutes before bedtime we can take a look.'

June had a simply enormous collection of trick booklets, and she was forever studying them, and sending away for sneezing powder, or invisible ink, or some other ingenious product which she could use to trick the hapless Mam'zelle. As Miss Potts, the stern head of North Tower, remarked, 'If June put half as much energy into her school work as she does into her jokes and tricks, she would probably be the most brilliant pupil Malory Towers has ever had!'

But June, with her quick brains and amazing memory, managed to do extremely well at her schoolwork with the minimum of effort. It was very galling, both to the mistresses, and to the other girls, who had to work far harder to obtain respectable marks. And, of course, it meant that June could reserve all of her energy for games, jokes and tricks, all of which she was superlative at.

The third formers trooped up to the dormitory ten minutes before the bell for bedtime went – which surprised Matron very much!

'Hmm,' she said suspiciously to Mam'zelle Dupont. 'It's most unlike the third formers to go to bed early! I hope that they aren't planning a midnight feast, or some other mischief! I shall check on them later.'

But when Matron quietly opened the door of the third-form dormitory shortly after midnight, all of the girls were fast asleep. For, of course, the mischief that they had been planning had nothing to do with a feast!

The girls had gathered round as June produced a bewildering array of jokes and tricks from her bedside cabinet.

'My word, June!' exclaimed Lucy. 'You must spend all of your pocket money on this stuff. Why, there's enough here to start your own shop!'

'Itching powder!' cried Nora, snatching up a small pot. 'Goodness, just imagine poor old Mam'zelle Dupont scratching away for all she's worth!'

'I have something better in mind than that,' said June, rummaging around in her cabinet. 'Ah, here it is!'

She stood up, a small box in her hand and Felicity peered over her shoulder, reading aloud, 'Disappearing chalk. I say, that sounds exciting! How does it work, June?'

Grinning, June took what appeared to be an ordinary stick of chalk from the box, and answered, 'Well, it works in a similar way to the invisible ink that I used on Julie in the second form. Remember that, Julie?'

'I remember all right!' said Julie darkly. 'Miss Parker gave me some lines to do, for talking in class,' she explained to the new girls. 'But dear June filled up my pen with her invisible ink, so that by the time I got to the end of the page, the lines that I had written at the top had disappeared!'

The others laughed as they recalled the trick and Pam said, 'It took you all evening to write those lines, until June finally confessed what she had done.'

'Yes, I was simply furious at the time, though I saw the funny side afterwards,' grinned Julie. 'But the ink wasn't completely invisible, was it, June? I seem to remember that if you looked at the writing in a dark room and shone a torch on it, you could see it.'

'That's right,' said June. 'Well, the chalk works in a similar way. When someone writes on a blackboard with this, it works just like normal chalk. But, after a few minutes, it disappears and the board appears blank again. Just watch!'

And, under the astonished gaze of the third formers, June scrawled a big, white zig-zag pattern on the door of her cabinet. Everyone stared at it, then Nora cried, 'It's beginning to fade! Look!'

So it was, and after a few minutes, there was no trace of the pattern at all.

Freddie, her lively mind seeing all sorts of possibilities, gave a laugh and said, 'We can trick Mam'zelle properly with this. Let's make some plans!'

So the third formers plotted and schemed, and Felicity even allowed the rule about no talking after lights-out to be broken, though she was normally very strict about sticking to it.

'Only for a few minutes, though – and for goodness' sake keep your voices down,' she warned. 'If any of the mistresses come along and hear us we shall be in hot water.'

By the time the girls were ready to settle down to sleep, their plans had been made, and it was arranged that the trick would be played on Mam'zelle Dupont in French class the following morning.

Just before Mam'zelle arrived to take the lesson, June

went up to the blackboard and removed the chalk that was on the ledge, replacing it with a stick of her own special chalk.

'Quickly!' hissed Freddie, who was keeping watch at the classroom door. 'Back to your seat, June. I can hear Mam'zelle coming.'

The little French mistress always wore high-heeled shoes, which made a tip-tapping sound as she walked, so that the girls could hear her approaching, which proved very useful on occasions such as this!

Swiftly, June slipped back to her seat, while Freddie remained by the door, holding it open for Mam'zelle to enter.

'*Merci*, Freddie,' said the French mistress, beaming round at the class. '*Bonjour, mes enfants*. Please sit down.'

Mam'zelle Dupont was in a very good mood. Yesterday, as the wicked June knew, she had been to the opticians to get some new spectacles, and she was very pleased with them indeed. The tortoiseshell frames were, thought Mam'zelle, *très chic*, and so much more attractive than her old black ones. Ah, and the dear girls, they had noticed the change in their old Mam'zelle's appearance too, for they were smiling at her in approval. Well, of course, the third formers were smiling in anticipation of the trick that was about to be played, but Mam'zelle had no idea of this and was happy. Especially when Bonnie, who was one of her favourites, said in her pretty, lisping voice, 'Oh, Mam'zelle, how lovely you look in your new glasses!'

Mam'zelle's smile grew even wider and she cried, 'Ah,

you flatter me, *ma chère*! Now, you will bring your books to me one at a time please, and I shall correct your prep. Nora, you first.'

'Heavens, I hope Mam'zelle isn't going to spend too long looking at everyone's prep,' whispered Freddie to June. 'Or we shan't have time to play the trick. Nora! Make sure that you don't keep her talking for too long!'

Nora was another of Mam'zelle's favourites, and the girl had a trick of engaging the French mistress in conversation whenever she took her book up for correction. Normally the third formers were happy to encourage this, as it wasted a great deal of the lesson, but today they wanted to get their prep marked as quickly as possible. So Nora was not as chatty as usual, and was back at her desk in no time at all. Soon Mam'zelle had looked at everyone's work, and she got to her feet. The French mistress usually began the class by setting a few questions, and she then went round the class asking for answers. She stuck to her routine today, saying, 'Now, I will test your French grammar by writing down some simple questions on the blackboard, in French. You will answer them orally, also in French, *n'est-ce pas*?'

Then Mam'zelle turned to the blackboard, picked up June's disappearing chalk and began writing. Nora wanted to laugh already, even though the trick hadn't begun yet, and she clamped a hand firmly across her mouth, while Julie and Lucy grinned at one another in anticipation. What a super trick this was going to be!

The girls were busily scribbling down the questions as

fast as Mam'zelle was writing them on the blackboard. They had to be sure to copy every word before the chalk disappeared, otherwise the trick would not work. By the time Mam'zelle finished writing the last question, the first one had already began to fade a little and, to distract the French mistress, Susan put up her hand and asked, 'Mam'zelle, are we to write down the answers to the questions, or do you want us to answer them orally?'

Mam'zelle looked at Susan in surprise and said, 'Why, you will speak your answers, of course, Susan. Have I not just said so?'

'Oh, did you, Mam'zelle?' said Susan meekly. 'Sorry, I wasn't concentrating.'

'This is not like you, Susan,' said Mam'zelle, a little sternly. 'Now, you shall answer the first question, and you will pay attention, *d'accord*?'

'*Oui*, Mam'zelle,' answered Susan seriously, glancing over the French mistress's shoulder and seeing that the blackboard was now quite blank.

'*Bien!*' said Mam'zelle, 'Now, the first question is . . .'

Mam'zelle turned to face the blackboard, giving such a start of surprise that her brand-new glasses slid down her nose. '*Tiens!*' she cried. 'My questions, they have vanished.'

'Whatever do you mean, Mam'zelle?' asked Susan, feigning a puzzled look.

'See for yourself!' exclaimed Mam'zelle, becoming agitated as she flung her arm out towards the blackboard. 'I wrote them carefully on the blackboard, and now they are gone!'

The rest of the third formers pretended to look very puzzled too, all except Nora, who could feel a terrific snort of laughter coming on and quickly lifted the lid of her desk so that she could hide behind it.

'Gone, Mam'zelle?' said June. 'Whatever do you mean? Why, the questions are there on the blackboard as plain as day. We can all see them, can't we, girls?'

The third formers all nodded and Mam'zelle cried, 'Ah, this is a treek! June, if the questions are there on the blackboard then read me the first one!'

June, who had memorised the first question so that she did not need to glance at her notebook, peered at the blackboard and read it out. Her expression was so grave and earnest that it proved too much for Nora, who gave one of her explosive snorts of laughter, which she hurriedly turned into a cough.

'You, Nora!' said Mam'zelle. 'You read me the second question.'

Nora, whose memory was not as good as June's, glanced quickly down at the paper on her desk where she had scribbled the questions, and repeated it rather hesitantly, mispronouncing a couple of words. Fortunately, she was poor at French anyway, so Mam'zelle did not notice anything out of the ordinary!

'It is a treek,' she muttered to herself. 'Either that, or my poor eyes are deceiving me!'

The French mistress asked Amy, Felicity and Susan to read out the next three questions, which they all did most convincingly, so that poor Mam'zelle was quite at a loss.

She walked up to the blackboard and ran her hand across it, then examined it from all angles, her expression of bewilderment so comical that several of the girls found it hard to contain their laughter.

'Perhaps it is something to do with your new spectacles, Mam'zelle,' suggested Pam.

The French mistress considered this, taking off her new glasses and looking at them closely. But that was no good at all, for without them Mam'zelle could hardly see a thing! She put them back on again, just in time to see June waving at someone through the open window – but there was no one there!

'June!' she called sharply. 'Who do you wave to?'

'Why, it's Amanda from the sixth form,' answered the wicked June. 'Look, there she is, over by the flower beds. Hi, Amanda!'

June leaned out of the window, waving frantically and Mam'zelle, fearing for her sanity now, cried, 'But there is no one there!'

'It's Amanda all right, as large as life,' said Freddie, also leaning out of the window. 'Coo-ee! Amanda!'

This was the signal for all the girls who were seated by the windows to begin waving furiously, all of them shouting to attract the attention of the non-existent Amanda, and soon the noise became quite deafening.

'Silence!' shouted Mam'zelle, covering her hands with her ears. 'Back to your seats at once!'

But, before the girls could sit down, the door opened and Miss Potts appeared. She had been taking the first formers in the classroom next door, and wondered what on earth was going on in Mam'zelle's class! The third formers were making so much noise that she could barely hear herself think!

The mistress pursed her lips as she took in the scene before her. Half of the third formers seemed to be hanging out of the windows yelling themselves hoarse, while the other half watched, with tears of laughter running down their cheeks. As for Mam'zelle herself, her attempts to restore order were having no effect at all!

Miss Potts raised her voice and said sharply, 'Mam'zelle Dupont! What is the meaning of all this noise?'

No one had heard Miss Potts enter, and Mam'zelle wheeled round sharply, the girls at the windows returning quickly to their seats, some of them looking a little scared.

'Ah, Miss Potts!' cried Mam'zelle. 'My eyes, they have gone wrong! The girls, they wave to that big Amanda, but I cannot see her!'

Miss Potts marched over to the nearest window and looked out. 'Mam'zelle, you can't see Amanda because she isn't there. June!'

June jumped at the sharpness of Miss Potts's tone and, turning slightly red, said, 'Yes, Miss Potts?'

'Was Amanda outside?'

'Well, I *thought* that I saw her,' said June, not wanting to tell an outright lie to the mistress. 'But I think that she's gone now.'

Before Miss Potts could reply to this, Mam'zelle claimed her attention again, crying, 'But that is not all, Miss Potts.

I cannot see the writing on the blackboard either. There is something wrong with my eyes, I tell you!'

Miss Potts looked at the blackboard and then at Mam'zelle Dupont, wondering if the French mistress was in her right mind that morning, and said crisply, 'Well, there is nothing wrong with *my* eyes, Mam'zelle, and I can see no writing on the blackboard either.'

Mam'zelle stared at Miss Potts and said, 'But this is impossible! The dear girls, they can see the writing.'

'Can they indeed?' said Miss Potts, sounding very sceptical indeed. 'I think, Mam'zelle, that the girls have been playing a trick on you. No doubt June or Freddie will be happy to explain it to you!'

And with that, Miss Potts stalked from the room, leaving the girls staring at one another apprehensively, while Mam'zelle stood in the middle of the floor, her mouth agape. At last she found her voice, and cried, 'So, June! And you, Freddie! Once again you have tricked your old Mam'zelle. You will please explain to me how it was done.'

So the two girls went to the front of the class, and while June explained to Mam'zelle how the disappearing chalk worked, Freddie demonstrated by writing her name on the blackboard.

Mam'zelle watched intently, and Felicity grinned to herself as she realised that Mam'zelle's anger was giving way to enjoyment, as the French mistress exclaimed over the ingenuity of the trick.

'*Oh là là!*' she exclaimed. 'See how the writing fades!

And now he has disappeared altogether. It is a most marvellous treek indeed!'

Then she made her expression very stern as she turned to face June and Freddie, saying, 'Of course, I must confiscate this chalk at once.'

'Yes, Mam'zelle,' chorused both girls meekly.

'I shall take it with me when I go to France in the holidays,' went on Mam'zelle, the stern look vanishing as she beamed. 'My sister teaches the *petits enfants* at the school in our village, you see, and I shall play a treek on her! How *les petits* will laugh when they see her writing vanish before their eyes!'

And how the girls laughed. What a sport old Mam'zelle was!

'Thank goodness that Mam'zelle Dupont has a sense of humour,' said Freddie to June later. 'If we had played that trick on any other mistress in the school we would be in real trouble. It was a jolly good trick, though, wasn't it?'

'I'll say!' said June, with a grin. 'And it has put me in the mood to play a few more!'

Tricks and tennis

Miss Potts, who knew Mam'zelle Dupont well, was not surprised to hear her squealing with laughter shortly after she had left the third form's classroom. And although Miss Potts couldn't help smiling to herself at Mam'zelle's little ways, she shook her head as well.

'I sincerely hope that you have punished those two girls, Mam'zelle,' she said to the French mistress later, in the mistresses' common-room.

'Of course,' said Mam'zelle, with great dignity. 'I confiscated the trick chalk that they used, and I scolded them most severely. The poor June was almost in tears.'

'Really?' said Miss Potts, disbelievingly, quite unable to picture Mam'zelle reducing anyone – let alone the brazen June – to tears.

Then the French mistress began to chuckle. 'Ah, it was a very funny treek they played on me, those wicked girls! That June, she is so clever.'

'Very clever and very naughty!' said Miss Potts, sternly. 'If you were a little firmer with her, Mam'zelle, she might not be encouraged to think that she can get away with anything!'

And, indeed, it seemed that June *did* think that she

could get away with anything, for she and Freddie went 'trick-mad', as Felicity called it, over the next few days. They made Bonnie squeal by putting insects in her pencil case, infuriated Amy by replacing her expensive talcum powder with itching powder, and ruined Felicity and Susan's tennis practice by substituting a trick ball for the real one.

June also managed to sneak a bottle of invisible ink into Eleanor Banks's satchel, laughing as she said to Freddie, 'I'd love to see Miss James's face when Eleanor hands her prep in, after she's used my special ink!'

But Felicity called the two to order after they put a frog in Esme's bed, and the girl screamed so loudly that both Matron and Miss Peters appeared on the scene. Neither of the grown-ups was amused at being dragged from their beds, but they accepted Esme's explanation that she had had a nightmare. And Esme went up in everyone's estimation for not sneaking on the two culprits, for she hated frogs and really had been very frightened indeed.

Lucy, with her mother's letter in mind, went up to her cousin the next morning and said, 'It was jolly decent of you not to split on June and Freddie.'

Esme, surprised and rather pleased at being spoken to in such a friendly way by Lucy, smiled and said, 'Well, I didn't want to get them into trouble. And they only meant it as a joke – I guess they weren't to know that I'm scared stiff of frogs!'

'I don't much like them either,' said Lucy, with a shudder. 'But of course, you know that already, don't you?

Do you remember that time when we were little and we found one by the pond in your garden?'

Bonnie and Julie, standing nearby, exchanged glances and Julie said in a low voice, 'Let's hope that this is the start of a better understanding between those two.'

Bonnie nodded and said, 'It must be difficult for both of them, after what's happened in the past.'

'Oh, so Esme told you about that, did she?' said Julie. 'Lucy confided in me as well.'

'Hmm,' said Bonnie, looking thoughtful. 'It's an awful shame. If only we could think of a way to get the family back together again. If you ask me –'

'Hush!' hissed Julie. 'They're coming over, and they won't be very pleased if they think that we have been gossiping about their private business.'

So Bonnie immediately changed the subject and began talking about the forthcoming half-term.

'I'm so looking forward to it,' said Julie, as Lucy and Esme joined them. 'My parents and brother are coming on horseback, and we're going for a picnic on the cliff-tops.'

'How super!' said Lucy enviously. 'My mother will be coming alone on the Saturday, as Father can't get away until Sunday. She doesn't care for horses, I'm afraid, so I won't be getting such a marvellous treat! I expect we'll be going to a restaurant instead.'

'Well, I think that's much nicer than a picnic, with the sun ruining your complexion, and insects buzzing around all the time,' said Bonnie. 'What about you, Esme? Are your parents coming?'

'I don't know yet,' said Esme. 'They're going on holiday the week before and they may not be back in time. I sure hope they can make it, though.'

All of the girls were looking forward to half-term enormously. Most of them had parents, or brothers and sisters, coming to take them out for the day, and to watch the tennis and swimming displays.

Felicity and Susan were both taking part in the diving, while June had been chosen to play against one of the fourth formers in an exhibition tennis match.

'It's a tremendous honour for the third, June,' Felicity told her, when they were in the courtyard one day. 'You're the only girl in the school who is playing against someone from a higher form. Has Amanda told you who you're going to be playing against yet?'

'Well, it was to have been Penelope Turner, but she sprained her wrist last week,' said June. 'So if she's not fully recovered, I shall be playing Hilda Fenwick instead.'

'Golly!' said Susan, coming up just in time to hear this. 'Penelope's a marvellous player, but Hilda is quite superb – and very aggressive! She came jolly close to beating Amanda herself once, and no one else has ever done that before. I hope for your sake, June, that Penelope is better in time.'

'Well, I'd rather play Hilda, thank you very much!' retorted June. 'And I'd rather lose against her than beat Penelope.'

'You must be mad!' said Susan roundly. 'Just think of the glory that you would bring to the third form if you beat Penelope.'

'To my mind, there's not much glory in beating someone who has just recovered from an injury,' said June. 'If I win against Penelope, people will say that she only lost because her wrist wasn't quite right. Now if I'm up against Hilda, I can really give it everything I've got. And, win or lose, no one will be able to say I didn't do my very best and put up a good fight.'

'Well!' said Susan, as June went off to find Freddie. 'Wonders will never cease! If anyone had told me a few terms ago that June would one day go all out to win a tennis match for the honour of her form, I would have said that they were quite mad.'

Felicity laughed, but said thoughtfully, 'Do you really think that she's doing it for the third form, Susan? Or for herself?'

'Whatever do you mean?' asked Susan.

'Well, June has certainly knuckled down to swimming and tennis since Amanda started taking an interest in her. But those are sports where one plays as an individual, and not as part of a team. And June still doesn't have any team spirit. Do you remember what happened when Amanda put her in the lacrosse team last term?'

'Yes,' said Susan. 'We drew, when we could so easily have won. Because June was determined to shoot a goal herself and hogged the ball. Elizabeth Jenkins from West Tower was in a perfect position to shoot in the last few minutes, and would probably have won the match for us. But June simply had to try and score herself, even though she was too far away.'

'Exactly!' said Felicity. 'June wanted to be the heroine of the hour, and that was more important to her than whether the team won or lost. Miss Maxwell was absolutely furious with her, and gave her a thorough ticking off afterwards.'

'I remember,' said Susan. 'But Amanda didn't scold her at all. I thought at the time that it was rather odd.'

'I overheard Amanda talking to Kay Foster about it afterwards,' Felicity said. 'She was frightfully disappointed that Malory Towers hadn't won the match, but she told Kay that she understood exactly how June felt. Amanda said that she had been just the same when she was training for the Olympics, and that she had always gone in for swimming and tennis because she didn't want anyone else sharing in her glory.'

'Golly!' exclaimed Susan. 'But old Amanda has plenty of team spirit now. Miss Grayling wouldn't have made her games captain otherwise.'

'Yes,' said Felicity. 'But she told Kay that she had only learned to play as part of a team since coming here. Which doesn't surprise me at all! If you have any team spirit in you at all, then good old Malory Towers is the place to bring it out.'

'Well, let's just hope that June has some team spirit in *her*!' said Susan. 'She still has a few years in which to find it.'

But, for now, June was concentrating solely on her tennis, determined to make a good showing at half-term and in the match against St Margaret's. She spent every spare moment on the tennis court, badgering Freddie, or Felicity, or Susan into going with her so that she had someone to practise against.

'My word, she's good!' said Penelope Turner to her friend Meg, as they watched June playing against Felicity one afternoon. 'I almost hope that my wrist doesn't get better in time for half-term! Imagine the humiliation of being beaten by one of those third-form kids!'

Someone else who was devoting a lot of time to tennis, much to the astonishment of the third form, was Esme. The girl had finally 'confessed', as she put it, to Amy and Bonnie that she was to be reserve for the tennis matches, and had been unsurprised at their reaction.

'Oh dear!' Amy had said, looking most dismayed. 'Please tell me that you aren't becoming one of these dreadful, sporting types, like Felicity, or that big, ungainly Amanda Chartelow.' Amy shuddered and went on, 'She's so loud and aggressive that I simply can't bear her. And she looks more like a boy than a girl.'

'I blame myself,' Bonnie had said sorrowfully. 'I should have thought of a way to get you out of tennis practice earlier. Perhaps it's not too late, Esme. Let me have a think and I'll see if I can come up with a plan.'

'Yes, but the thing is,' Esme had said, rather hesitantly, 'I – I don't actually *want* to get out of it. You see, until I came to Malory Towers, I didn't even *know* that I could play tennis. I've never really been good at anything before and – well, I actually feel quite proud of myself. Not only that, but I'm enjoying it as well.'

Amy looked quite horrified at this, but the more large-minded Bonnie said, 'It seems very queer to me, but I suppose if that's the way you feel there's nothing we can do about it. You must promise that you won't go all tomboyish on us, though. In fact, Esme, I think it's your duty to show Amanda and the rest of them that it's possible to play sport and still be feminine and pretty and graceful.'

'Yes, I'll do that,' Esme had agreed, relieved that Bonnie, at least, seemed to be taking the news quite well.

Amy, however, remained extremely disapproving and after Esme had left the common-room she said to Bonnie, 'I feel quite let down by Esme, when I think of all the help that we tried to give her. I don't know that I want to be friends with her any more.'

Amy sounded rather petulant, and Bonnie, picking up her sewing, smiled to herself. She knew that Amy had only befriended Esme because she thought that the American girl admired and looked up to her, and didn't have much genuine liking or affection for her at all. Attempting to turn Esme into a replica of herself had been more for her own gratification than the other girl's. And Amy's conceit made it difficult for her to accept that Esme was beginning to realise that she didn't *want* to be just like her.

Bonnie, for her part, genuinely liked Esme and, although she missed seeing so much of her, now that tennis was taking up a lot of her time, she was pleased that Esme had found an activity that she enjoyed. Unlike Amy,

Bonnie was interested in people, and her sympathy had been stirred by Esme's story of her family's quarrel. How she hoped that the two fathers would be able to put their differences behind them!

Esme, meanwhile, went off to her tennis practice. The good-hearted Freddie, overcoming her own disappointment at not being chosen as reserve, selflessly gave up her time so that the others could practise with her. Today, she and Esme were playing doubles against Felicity and Susan. The weather was extremely warm, and by the end of the first set all four girls felt uncomfortably hot.

'Phew!' said Freddie, flopping down on the grass and fanning herself with her racket. 'I'm worn out after just one set!'

'Me too,' said a red-faced Susan. 'I'm roasting! Perhaps we should stop now.'

Felicity frowned at this suggestion, but it was Esme who surprised everyone, saying bracingly, 'Nonsense! If we were playing in a tournament we wouldn't be able to stop after one set, simply because we felt hot and tired. I say that we should play on.'

'Hear, hear!' said Felicity. 'Come on, we'll have a drink of lemonade and then we'll all feel as right as rain.'

The girls had all brought bottles of lemonade with them, and they moved to the side of the court now, drinking thirstily. Felicity was right, and they all felt refreshed once their thirst had been quenched, playing on with new heart.

Felicity and Susan won the match, but it was a close

thing. As they walked off the court, Felicity said to Susan, 'I think Freddie was off her game a little today, otherwise we might have lost. Esme played superbly.'

'Didn't she just!' said Susan. 'Who would have thought, at the beginning of term, that she had it in her?'

'She really seems to be finding her feet at Malory Towers,' said Felicity, pleased. 'Doing well at tennis seems to have given her confidence in other ways. She doesn't copy Amy so much now, and she's trying much harder at her lessons. If she carries on like this, there's a chance that she might go up into the fifth form next term, while we go into the fourth.'

'Golly, that would be a shame,' said Susan, looking a little dismayed. 'A shame for us, I mean, though of course it would be a jolly good thing for Esme. I suppose that Lucy will be pleased to see the back of her too.'

'Perhaps, although the two of them do seem to be making an effort and getting on a little better now,' said Felicity. 'In fact, the only fly in the ointment at the moment seems to be this beastly business with Bill and Clarissa.'

'I shall be glad when Bill's arm is better,' said Susan. 'What with helping out at Five Oaks, tennis, swimming and lessons I feel absolutely exhausted!'

'Yes, it's been quite a busy term,' agreed Felicity. 'We shall all be jolly glad of a break when half-term comes.'

The girls were so busy that the last few days before half-term simply flew by. Then on Saturday morning, Felicity woke early. She knew that she was excited about something, but at first she couldn't think what it was. Then a little thrill of joy ran through her as she remembered, and she sat up in bed.

'Wake up, everyone!' she cried happily. 'It's half-term!'

A super half-term

The parents seemed to arrive slowly at first – in 'dribs and drabs', as Pam said. Then, as the morning wore on, more and more arrived, and soon the grounds were filled with groups of laughing, chattering girls and their families. Felicity was thrilled that her mother and father were among the first to arrive. She flew to meet them, hugging first her mother, then her father.

'Did you get my letter, Mother?' she asked eagerly. 'I'm taking part in the diving later, and so is Susan.'

'Yes, I got it, dear,' said Mrs Rivers, beaming happily at her excited daughter. 'Daddy and I were awfully proud to hear that you had been chosen. So was Darrell, of course. She telephoned me the other evening, and said to wish you luck.'

'How I wish that she could have come with you!' said Felicity.

'Well, she's working awfully hard at the moment,' said Mr Rivers. 'But the summer holidays aren't too far away, so you will see one another then.'

Nearby, Felicity could see Pam with her parents, and Nora with her mother and young sister. And in the distance she could see Susan, chattering nineteen-to-the-dozen with her big, jolly father, while Bonnie enjoyed being fussed over by her doting parents.

I wonder if Esme's parents are here too? thought Felicity. I do hope so.

Sadly for Esme, they weren't. She had received a message to say that her parents wouldn't be returning from their trip until late this afternoon, by which time it would be too late for them to travel to Malory Towers. But they meant to set off early the following morning, so that she would be able to spend tomorrow with them. All the same, the girl couldn't help feeling a little forlorn as she saw the happy time that the others were having. There was Julie, dressed in her riding gear, ready to go off with her parents and brother for their picnic. And there – looking so like her beloved mother that Esme gave a gasp – was Aunt Janet, with Lucy. Esme hadn't seen her aunt since the families fell out, and for a moment she stood rooted to the spot, hardly knowing what to do. But the problem was solved by her aunt, who spotted Esme and came over at once, a delighted smile on her face.

'Esme, my dear!' she said, kissing the girl on the cheek. 'How wonderful to see you again.'

'Hallo, Aunt Janet,' answered Esme, her voice a little shaky. 'I'm so pleased that you could come and see Lucy.'

Lucy, who had been hovering a little awkwardly in the background, said, 'I was just telling Mother that you weren't sure whether your people would be able to come, Esme.'

'No, they telephoned Miss Grayling this morning and

said that they wouldn't be able to get here today,' said Esme. 'But they are coming tomorrow.'

'Well, that's good,' said Mrs Carstairs. 'But you can't possibly stay here alone today, while everyone else is off enjoying themselves. I insist that you come out to lunch with Lucy and me.'

Esme glanced at her cousin, sure that she wouldn't be too happy about the invitation, but Lucy was smiling. So Esme smiled too, and said happily, 'Thank you, Aunt Janet. That *will* be a treat after I was expecting to stay here for school lunch.'

The restaurant that Mrs Carstairs took the girls to was a very good one, and they had a slap-up meal. But, even more than the delicious food, Esme enjoyed the company of her aunt and cousin. There were a few awkward moments when the girls mentioned their fathers, but on the whole they had a very pleasant time, recalling childhood incidents and telling Lucy's mother about life at Malory Towers. Mrs Carstairs teased Esme good-naturedly about her American accent and Lucy laughed, saying, 'You should have heard it when she first started at Malory Towers, Mother. It was much stronger then.'

'Was it really?' said Esme, looking surprised.

'Oh yes,' said Lucy. 'You seem to have lost some of it as the term has gone on. And you don't say "gee" half as much as you used to. Why, at times you sound quite English!'

'Heavens!' exclaimed Esme. 'Mother *will* be pleased.'

'How is your mother, Esme?' asked Mrs Carstairs, looking rather wistful. 'I do miss her terribly, you know.'

'Well, I know that she misses you as well,' said Esme. 'But you'll be able to see her tomorrow. Perhaps the two of you could talk, and –'

But Lucy's mother shook her head, regretfully. 'I only wish that we could, my dear. But your father will be there, and Lucy's father is hoping to come tomorrow as well, so that might make things a little awkward.'

Both girls looked uncomfortable now, so Mrs Carstairs hastily changed the subject, saying, 'Well, we've a little time to spare before the diving and swimming at Malory Towers, so what would you girls like to do now?'

They thought for a moment, then Esme said, 'Why don't we pop over to Five Oaks and see Sandy? I never did get to say hallo to him.'

Lucy, of course, was only too happy to agree to this, so her mother said, 'Very well. As long as you don't try to get me up on his back, Lucy! You know that I'm not a great one for horses.'

Julie and her people were also at Five Oaks, returning Jack to his stable after their picnic. There was a flurry of introductions, then, while Julie's mother chatted with Mrs Carstairs, Esme spotted Sandy, who had poked his head out of his stall to see what all the noise was about.

'Sandy!' she cried joyfully, going up to stroke the horse's nose. 'How marvellous to see you again, boy.'

Sandy whinnied softly and nudged Esme, who laughed and said, 'I really believe that he remembers me!'

'Perhaps he does,' said Lucy, with a smile.

Just then Bill and Clarissa appeared, and there were

yet more introductions, for neither Esme nor Mrs Carstairs had met the two girls before. Esme, who had heard so much about them that she felt as if she knew them very well indeed, looked at Bill and Clarissa with interest. Bill's arm was still in plaster, and she said, 'I have to go back to the hospital next week, and I'm hoping that the doctor will say that the plaster can come off. And won't I be glad when I can get up on old Thunder again! Not being able to ride has been simply dreadful for both of us!'

Soon it was time for the Malory Towers girls and their families to return to the school in time for the swimming and tennis, but before they left, Julie found an opportunity to take Clarissa aside.

'I don't seem to have had the chance to talk to you or Bill in private just lately,' she said. 'How are things? Have there been any more strange happenings?'

'No, thank heavens,' said Clarissa. 'Jim did catch a strange man prowling round here the other night, just before he went home for the evening. But he turned out to be one of Mr Banks's grooms. Mr Banks had sent him over to have a scout round and check that everything was all right.'

'That was thoughtful of him,' said Julie.

'Yes, he's been very good to us,' said Clarissa. 'Of course, Bill knows now that her "accident" was no accident. Now that she's feeling stronger, I thought it best to tell her so that she could be on her guard.'

'Good idea,' said Julie. 'Although it sounds as if

whoever was behind it may have decided to stop these rotten tricks.'

'I certainly hope so,' said Clarissa, with a sigh. 'It's been an awfully difficult time. Of course, we've tried to keep the whole business quiet, but somehow word has got out and some of the children from the village have stopped coming for riding lessons. Their parents are afraid that they may be hurt too, so they won't allow the children to come until they're certain that it's quite safe.'

'Oh, Clarissa!' cried Julie in dismay. 'I had no idea.'

'Well, I suppose one can't blame them,' said Clarissa, suddenly looking rather strained. 'But of course, it means that we don't have as much money coming in as we used to.'

Julie, guessing that Clarissa was a lot more worried than she was letting on, said stoutly, 'Well, you may be sure that all the Malory Towers girls will continue to come, Clarissa. We'll stand by you all right!'

But Julie wished that there was something else that she, and the others, could do to help Bill and Clarissa. She would bring it up after half-term, for she certainly didn't want to dampen everyone's spirits today, of all days.

And what a marvellous day it was!

All of the girls had been taken out to lunch by their parents, though those who were taking part in the sports that afternoon had been careful not to eat too much.

'I shall make up for it at tea-time,' Felicity had said to her mother, after refusing an ice-cream. 'Half-term teas are always absolutely super!'

Indeed they were, and the kitchen staff had worked very hard at producing scores of dainty sandwiches, cakes, scones and big bowls of fat, juicy strawberries with jugs of cream.

But first there were the tennis and swimming exhibitions. Chairs had been arranged around the tennis court, and June's parents sat proudly at the front.

June herself felt a little nervous – a most unusual thing for her – as she watched the upper-school matches and waited for her turn to come. Her opponent was to be Hilda Fenwick, after all, and – for a fleeting moment – June found herself wishing that the less aggressive Penelope was playing instead. Then she spotted Hilda, chatting with one of her friends. The fourth former saw June watching her, and gave her a scornful smirk before turning back and saying something that made her friend laugh. At once June's moment of self-doubt vanished, her fighting spirit coming to the surface again. So, Hilda thought that she was going to have a walk-over, did she? Well, she could jolly well think again!

Felicity and her parents were sitting with Susan and her people to watch the match, and, as June and Hilda walked on to the court, Felicity whispered to Susan, 'My word! Just look at June's face!'

June wore an expression of grim determination, and even Hilda looked a little taken aback as the two girls faced one another.

Miss Maxwell, who was acting as umpire, tossed to see who would serve first. June won, and the two girls took their places. Then Miss Maxwell shouted, 'Play!' and the match began.

As there were several exhibition matches to get through, each one consisted of only one set. This meant that the spectators did not become bored and restless, and the players didn't get too tired. June, her nerves completely gone now, played her first game superbly, getting a couple of aces past the bigger girl and winning comfortably. But Hilda fought back, taking the second and, for a while, the games went with service.

It was a very exciting match, both girls going all out to win and fighting fiercely for each point, while their supporters cheered loudly and yelled encouragement.

June, though, had quickly discovered that Hilda's backhand was her weak point, and as the match went on she exploited this ruthlessly. And, as the score stood at five games to four in June's favour, her persistence paid off. Hilda faulted on her first service, and her second was more cautious. *Too* cautious, for June slammed the ball back, placing it where the fourth former couldn't hope to reach it.

'Love, fifteen,' called out Miss Maxwell, while the third formers yelled themselves hoarse.

'Good shot, June!'

'Go it, June!'

'You can do it, June! Play up!'

And June played up for all she was worth, winning the next two points. There was a tense silence as Hilda served to stay in the match. But alas, her nerve seemed to have deserted her completely and she muffed the service, placing the ball almost at June's feet. The girl could almost taste victory, and she hit the ball back so that it just cleared the net. Hilda, still at the baseline, ran forward, but it was no use. June had won! The third formers clapped and cheered, while June's parents beamed with pride.

The two girls walked to the net and shook hands, June saying, 'Bad luck, Hilda.'

'It wasn't bad luck,' said Hilda ruefully, gracious in defeat. 'I was completely outplayed. Jolly well done, June.'

'June played marvellously, didn't she?' said Susan to Felicity, as the two of them changed into their bathing costumes ready for the diving. 'I only hope that we do half as well!'

In fact the two of them did very well indeed, their display of diving very graceful and thrilling to watch. Felicity's beautiful swallow dive from the top board brought 'oohs' and 'aahs' from the first formers, and gasps of admiration from the parents. And Susan received a round of applause for her daring somersault, which she had practised to perfection.

'Simply marvellous, darling!' cried Mrs Rivers, when Felicity joined her parents afterwards.

'Yes, I was proud of you,' said Mr Rivers, giving her a hug. 'And I managed to take some good photographs as well. I shall send some to Darrell once I've had them developed.'

Then it was time for tea and, all too soon, it seemed, the

girls were waving their parents off. Most of them were staying in nearby hotels so that they could come back tomorrow, while others, who lived nearer to Malory Towers, were going home for the night.

'Well, what a perfectly super day!' said Nora, as the third formers gathered in the common-room.

'First-rate!' agreed Pam. 'And June beating Hilda at tennis, and Susan and Felicity doing so splendidly in the diving was the icing on the cake!'

'And talking of cakes, wasn't that a simply wizard tea?' said Freddie. 'I've eaten so much today that I feel as if I never want to eat again!'

'I daresay you'll feel differently tomorrow,' laughed Felicity.

'Ooh yes, we've still got tomorrow to look forward to!' cried Bonnie, clapping her hands together excitedly. 'How lovely!'

Even Amy, who usually found something to complain about, was in a good mood, for she had enjoyed spending the day with her parents and grandmother.

'I've had a marvellous time,' she said. 'I really think that this has been the most perfect day.'

'I'll second that!' said Esme. 'Thank you for asking me along today, Lucy. I enjoyed myself so much.'

'Well, it was really Mother who asked you,' said Lucy. 'But I'm glad that you came too.'

'It was so nice to see Aunt Janet again,' Esme said, rather wistfully. 'And it's perfectly obvious that she and Mother are missing one another terribly. If only there was something we could do to bring them together. And Father and Uncle Robert, of course.'

'Well, there isn't,' said Lucy, with a sigh. 'Quite frankly, Esme, I don't see how this rift between our parents is ever going to be mended!'

A family reunion

But Esme couldn't get the idea of out her head. If only she and Lucy could make things right, and the two families could be as one again, it would be too marvellous for words! 'Lucy, we must try to think of something!' she said, urgently. 'Tomorrow our parents are going to be here. It will be the first time that the four of them have been together, in the same place, for years. We just *can't* let this opportunity slip by!'

Lucy looked at her cousin thoughtfully for a moment then, at last, she said, 'You're right. Look here, I can't concentrate with all this excited chatter going on. Let's slip away, and find somewhere quiet where we shall be able to hear ourselves think.'

So the two girls slipped quietly from the room and went off to one of the little music rooms. Esme perched on the piano stool, while Lucy sat cross-legged on the floor, their brows creased with concentration as they thought hard.

'I'm quite certain that Mother and Aunt Maggie would be only too glad of an excuse to make up,' said Lucy. 'Our fathers are the ones that we need to get to work on. They're both so dreadfully stubborn!'

'And proud,' said Esme, with a sigh. Then her face lit up. 'What we need is a situation where they have to forget about their silly pride, because something more important is at stake. I know! Suppose we were to push one of them into the swimming-pool, so that the other had to come to his rescue?'

'That would never work,' said Lucy scornfully. 'Both of them swim like fish, and wouldn't need rescuing. All that would happen is that you and I would get into a dreadful row.'

'Yes, I suppose you're right,' said Esme, rather glumly. 'Oh dear, how difficult it all is!'

But Lucy suddenly snapped her fingers and cried, 'Wait! Perhaps we could do it another way. We can't push Father or Uncle Philip in – but you could pretend to *fall* in!'

'*Me?*' said Esme, looking quite alarmed. 'But what good would that do?'

'Don't you see?' said Lucy. 'You'll have to make some excuse to get away from your parents, and come down to the swimming-pool, where I will be waiting with mine. Then you must throw yourself in the deep end, and pretend that you're in difficulties. Of course, my father will dive in and rescue you. And *your* father will be so grateful to him that it will be quite impossible for the pair of them to carry on being enemies.'

Esme looked simply horrified at this, and said, 'Why can't *you* pretend to fall in, and *my* father can rescue you?'

'Because I swim like a fish too,' answered Lucy. 'What's the matter, Esme? Are you afraid of spoiling your hair?'

'No, I'm afraid of drowning!' retorted Esme, nettled by the scorn in her cousin's voice. 'Lucy, you know that I'm not a very good swimmer, and I always stay in the shallow end.'

'Yes, and that's why it will be so much more convincing if *you* pretend to fall in, rather than me!' said Lucy. 'And there's not the slightest chance of you drowning. Even if my father doesn't come to the rescue – which he most definitely will – I shall be there to haul you out.'

Esme digested this in silence for a moment, then said, 'But suppose someone else rescues me? That would simply ruin everything! It's half-term, remember, and there will be lots of people about.'

'Well, we shall just have to choose our time carefully,' said Lucy, looking thoughtful. 'I know! We'll do it at two o'clock. There's a gymnastics display on then, so most of the parents will be watching that. The whole thing will only take a few moments. Now, once my father has pulled you out of the pool, you will have to pretend to be unconscious for a few minutes. Meanwhile, I'll dash off to fetch your parents and tell them that Father has saved you from drowning. We'll have to exaggerate a bit, of course, so that Uncle Philip feels properly grateful. And once your parents arrive at the pool, you can pretend to come round, and tell them that you owe your life to Father. If that doesn't get them talking, I don't know what will!'

Esme still looked rather doubtful and Lucy said earnestly, 'Esme, if you find the courage to go through with this, it will be the bravest and best thing that you have ever done. Our families will be reunited, and it will be all thanks to you.'

Esme was much struck by this, but a little voice piped up at the back of her mind: what if it doesn't work? What if something goes wrong?

Yes, but what if I let the chance of ending this stupid feud pass by? thought Esme. What if my parents, and Lucy's, never speak to one another again, because I didn't have the pluck to go through with our plan? That would be far worse than trying and failing.

She took a deep breath and said, 'I'll do it.'

'Good for you!' said Lucy, getting up and clapping her cousin on the back. 'I say, if it all works out, perhaps our parents will decide to move next door to each other again. Won't that be fun?'

'I'll say,' said Esme, her face breaking into a smile. 'Things will be just as they used to be.'

But they wouldn't be *quite* the same, thought Lucy, sobering suddenly, for Julie was her best friend now. And Lucy had no intention of throwing her off. She was getting on with Esme very much better now than she had at the beginning of term, and the old fondness they had felt for one another was starting to come back – but her cousin would never take Julie's place with her. She wondered how she could broach this subject without offending Esme, but, almost as if the girl had read her mind, Esme said, 'Of course, I realise that things have changed. *We* have both changed a great deal over the years. And I know that Julie is your friend now. I certainly wouldn't try to come between you – the two of you get on so well together that it simply wouldn't be right. But it will be nice for the two of us to have one another for company in the holidays.'

'Oh yes, that would be super,' agreed Lucy, relieved that Esme understood and accepted the situation. Grinning, she added, 'Perhaps I can teach you to ride.'

'And perhaps I can teach you how to dress properly, and do your hair so that you don't look like a boy!' laughed Esme.

Just then the bell rang for bedtime and Lucy said, 'Heavens, I had no idea it was so late! We'd better dash. You know what a stickler Felicity is for putting the lights out on time.'

So the two girls made their way to the dormitory, both of them feeling excited and a little apprehensive. If only their scheme worked, then this would turn out to be the best half-term ever!

The third formers gathered in the common-room to wait for their people after breakfast on Sunday morning.

'Your parents won't arrive any sooner because you're standing there watching, you know,' June called out to Freddie, who had stationed herself at the window.

'I know, but I get so impatient and restless when I'm waiting for people,' sighed Freddie. 'I just can't seem to settle to anything. Oh, here comes a car! Does it belong to anyone here?'

'No, those are Kay Foster's parents,' said Felicity, going across to join Freddie. 'But a few more cars are coming.

Bonnie, I do believe one of them belongs to your people!'

As Bonnie gave a squeal and ran from the room, Freddie said, 'Your parents are here, too, Lucy – or are they Esme's? Your mothers look so alike that I can't tell one from the other!'

The two cousins went across to the window, and Esme said in a rather hollow voice, 'They're mine.'

'Well, you don't sound very pleased to see them!' said Nora, surprised.

In fact, Esme's feelings were very mixed. Of course she was pleased to see her parents, but she was also feeling extremely nervous about the scheme that she and Lucy had come up with. She glanced at her cousin, who gave her a reassuring smile, then went off to greet her parents. She was doing this for the good of the family, Esme reminded herself firmly, and if the plan failed it wouldn't be because of a lack of courage on her part!

Susan's parents weren't able to come that day, so she was going out with Felicity and her people. The two girls ran outside together to greet Mr and Mrs Rivers as soon as their car drew up, almost knocking over Eleanor Banks, who was standing at the bottom of the steps, talking to her uncle.

'Watch where you're going, you third formers!' she said crossly.

'Sorry, Eleanor!' chorused Susan and Felicity, both of them glancing at Mr Banks rather curiously. He was a tall man – very pale, like Eleanor herself – with hooded eyes and thin lips, which seemed to be curved into a permanent smile.

'Is that Eleanor's uncle?' murmured Felicity to Susan. 'He looks rather sinister, don't you think? I never trust people who smile all the time!'

Susan laughed and said, 'You shouldn't judge a book by its cover. Mr Banks has been jolly good to Bill and Clarissa in their time of need.'

'Of course, I had forgotten about that!' said Felicity. 'Well, he must be quite decent after all – and I suppose he can't help the way that he looks.'

Esme and Lucy, meanwhile, were having a grand time with their respective parents, though there was a tricky moment when the two families came face to face in the courtyard. The two mothers greeted one another rather awkwardly, while Mr Walters and Mr Carstairs merely nodded unsmilingly, and rather stiffly, before walking on. Lucy, unseen by the grown-ups, gave her cousin a wink, and Esme grinned back. Her father wouldn't be so stiff and unfriendly once he thought that Uncle Robert had saved her life!

But, once the time came for Esme to carry out her part in this daring plan, she didn't feel like grinning at all! There were butterflies in the girl's stomach as she led her parents to a bench, under the shade of a tree, in the courtyard. The grounds had been thronged with people earlier, but now it was quieter, for the gymnastics display was due to start shortly, and many of the parents had gone to watch.

'How pleasant it is just to sit quietly for a few moments,' said Mrs Walters. 'We have had such a busy morning, with so much to see. I must say, dear, Malory Towers seems a splendid school.'

'And that games mistress of yours was telling me that you're beginning to shine at tennis,' said Mr Walters, looking proudly at his daughter. 'It sure looks like this English school is bringing out some hidden talents in you.'

Normally, Esme would have basked in her parents' praise, but now she was on tenterhooks, for it was time for her to go down to the swimming-pool.

'Are you quite all right, dear?' asked her mother, looking at her in concern. 'You look a little flushed.'

'I'm fine, Mother,' said Esme. 'It's just that I'm a little hot and thirsty. I might go to the kitchen, and see if Cook can spare us some lemonade.'

'Good idea,' said her father. 'Shall I come and help you carry it?'

'Oh no, I can manage, Father,' Esme assured him hastily. 'You sit here and relax with Mother.'

And Esme walked off towards the kitchen, changing direction as soon as she was out of sight of her parents, and running off to the swimming-pool.

Lucy and her parents were already there, Lucy feeling quite as nervous as her cousin, now that the time had come for them to put their plan into action. She glanced round as Esme approached, but Mr and Mrs Carstairs had their backs to the girl, and didn't spot her until she was on the ledge of rocks surrounding the pool.

'Hallo, Esme!' said her aunt, sounding surprised. 'What are you doing here?'

'Oh, I – er – I thought I saw Felicity here,' answered Esme, a little flustered. 'I just needed to ask her something. Hallo, Uncle Robert.'

'Hallo, my dear,' answered her uncle, a little gruffly.

Lucy gave her cousin a meaningful look, which Esme knew meant that she was supposed to fall into the pool. But *how* was she to do it in a convincing way? If she just threw herself in, it wouldn't look realistic at all. As it turned out, though, Esme's fall was very realistic indeed! The rocks around the pool were extremely slippery and, as the girl stepped forward, her feet suddenly slid from under her, and she tumbled headlong into the pool, her scream of fright quite genuine.

Lucy stood rooted to the spot, as Esme disappeared under the water, while Mrs Carstairs gave a little cry of horror. And Mr Carstairs sprang into action immediately, throwing off his jacket and plunging into the pool after Esme. For a moment he, too, vanished beneath the surface, then he came up, gasping for air, an unconscious Esme in his arms.

'I think she may have banged her head on the rocks!' he called to his wife. 'Help me to get her out. And Lucy, run as fast as you can and find Esme's parents – and you'd better fetch Matron, too!'

Scared now, Lucy ran like the wind towards the school. *Why* had she thought up this stupid idea? If Esme turned out to be badly injured, it would all be her fault, and she would never forgive herself! And where on earth was she supposed to start looking for her aunt and uncle, for she didn't have the faintest idea where Esme had left them! Perhaps she had better go and fetch Matron first, for there was no time to waste. But, as she reached the courtyard, Lucy spotted her aunt and uncle sitting on a bench, and raced up to them.

'Why, Lucy!' said Mrs Walters, alarmed at the girl's panic-stricken expression. 'What on earth is the matter?'

'It – it's Esme,' gasped Lucy, trying to catch her breath. 'There's been an accident. She's fallen into the swimming-pool and hit her head.'

Mrs Walters turned pale, while Mr Walters was on his feet immediately, a look of horror on his face.

'My father dived in and pulled her out,' Lucy said. 'And he sent me to fetch you both, and Matron.'

'We shall go there at once,' said Mr Walters, trying to speak calmly, as he helped his wife to her feet. 'Lucy, you carry on and find Matron, will you? Tell her to come to the pool immediately. Good girl!'

Lucy sped off into the school, and up the stairs to Matron's room. She burst in, without pausing to knock, giving Matron a terrific start.

'My goodness!' she cried, looking most displeased at the third former's lack of manners. But before she could begin to scold, Lucy's face crumpled and, between sobs, she cried, 'Matron, you must come quickly! There's been a dreadful accident, and Esme is hurt.'

Matron was on her feet at once, putting a comforting arm about Lucy's shoulders, and saying in her brisk but kindly manner, 'There now, Lucy. Do try to keep calm, my

125

dear, or you won't be able to tell me what has happened. Take me to Esme, and you can explain what has happened on the way.'

But Matron and Lucy only got as far as the big hall when the door was suddenly opened and a very bedraggled Mr Carstairs appeared, followed by Mr Walters, who was carrying a pale, but conscious, Esme.

'Thank goodness!' breathed Lucy, while Matron took charge and said crisply, 'Bring her up to the San, Mr Walters. And Mr Carstairs, you had better get out of those wet things. Wait in my room, and I'll get someone to fetch you a blanket.'

With her usual efficiency, Matron soon had Esme undressed and in bed, where she examined her carefully. 'No bones broken, thank heavens,' she announced at last. 'But I'm afraid you're going to have a beautiful bruise on your forehead tomorrow, young lady!'

'I don't mind,' murmured Esme, a little smile on her lips. 'It was worth it.'

'Why, whatever do you mean?' asked Matron, astonished.

'I shouldn't be surprised if she was concussed,' said Lucy, hastily. 'I say, Matron, do you think I might have a word with Esme alone?'

Mr Walters frowned at this, and said, 'Gee, I don't know if that's a good idea, Lucy. Esme really needs some peace and quiet.'

But Esme said, 'It's all right, Father. I'd like to talk to Lucy. You and Mother will come and see me in a little while, won't you?'

'Just try to keep me away!' said her father.

'Don't keep Esme talking for too long, Lucy,' admonished Matron, as she ushered Mr Walters from the room. 'And now I'd better go and see how poor Mr Carstairs is doing.'

'I'll come with you, Matron,' the girls heard Esme's father say, as the door closed behind the two grown-ups. 'I've already shaken him by the hand once, but I need to do it again. He sure is a hero!'

'Did you hear that?' whispered Lucy gleefully. 'It worked! Esme, it worked!'

Esme smiled wanly and at once Lucy was contrite, saying, 'But I never meant you to get hurt, Esme. I wouldn't have had that happen for the world. I don't know about my father being a hero, but you're certainly a heroine.'

'No, I'm not,' said Esme, ruefully. 'I slipped and fell. So, you see, your father really *did* save my life!'

'But where are our mothers?' asked Lucy. 'I can't believe that they aren't here, at a time like this.'

'The last I saw of them, they were having a tearful reunion in the courtyard,' said Esme with a contented sigh. 'Though I daresay they will be here any minute. As soon as I came round, and Mother saw that I was going to be all right, she burst into tears. Of course, Aunt Janet comforted her, and before I knew what was happening, she was crying too, and the pair of them were hugging like nobody's business! As for my father, he simply couldn't thank Uncle Robert enough. Lucy, I do really think that everything will be all right now.'

So it seemed, for a moment later Matron bustled in, saying, 'I'm afraid I shall have to throw you out now, Lucy, for Esme's parents want to see her.'

'Darling, how are you feeling?' asked Mrs Walters, a very concerned look on her face as she entered the San.

'My head aches a bit, but I'll be all right,' answered Esme. 'I'm sorry to have given you both such a fright.'

'I'm just glad that your uncle was there,' said her father, gravely. 'I don't think I'll ever be able to thank him enough for saving you.'

'Does that mean that you're friends again now?' asked Esme hopefully.

'It sure does,' answered Mr Walters. 'I think what happened to you today made us realise how stubborn and foolish we had both been. But we won't let our pride get in the way of our friendship – or our families – again.'

'I'm so pleased to hear that,' said Esme contentedly. 'And I expect you are, too, aren't you, Mother?'

Mrs Walters nodded. 'I can't tell you how much I've missed my sister.'

'And Lucy and I are friends now, too,' said Esme. 'So everything has worked out perfectly. We're just one big, happy family again!'

Mam'zelle is a sport

The story of Esme's accident spread through the school like wildfire, and Lucy became quite embarrassed as one girl after another came up to her and congratulated her on her father's bravery.

'How lucky that he was there,' said Nora, in the common-room that evening.

'I'll say,' said Freddie, with a shudder. 'Just imagine what might have happened if no one had been around when Esme fell in.'

'You must be so proud of your father, Lucy,' said Felicity. 'I know I would be, if mine had done something so marvellous.'

'I saw your father and Esme's together at tea-time,' said Bonnie, staring hard at Lucy. 'The two of them were gabbling away nineteen-to-the-dozen. Just as if they were the best of friends.'

By now, the whole form knew the story of the feud between Lucy and Esme's family, and Susan said, 'Well, I should think it would be impossible for the two of them to remain enemies after what happened today. So at least something good has come out of it.'

Lucy turned red. Her father *had* been incredibly brave,

no doubt about it. But so had Esme, and it only seemed right and fair that the third formers should know it. So, taking a deep breath, she told the others the whole story of how she and Esme had planned the whole thing, to bring their families together.

'Well!' said Pam, looking quite astonished. 'Who would have thought that Esme would have the pluck to throw herself into the deep end.'

'As it turned out, she slipped and didn't need to throw herself in,' said Lucy. 'But she was quite ready to go through with it, so really, she was very brave as well.'

'Very brave and very foolish!' said Felicity, torn between admiration for Esme and horror at what could have happened. 'Heavens, she could have been seriously injured.'

'I know,' said Lucy, looking rather guilty. 'But thank goodness that she isn't. Matron says that she will be as right as rain in a day or two.'

To Esme's dismay, Matron insisted on keeping the girl in bed the following day.

'But I feel absolutely fine,' protested Esme. 'Really I do.'

After a dose of medicine and a good night's sleep, Esme's headache had completely vanished. As Matron had predicted, she had a simply enormous bruise on her forehead, and had been rather looking forward to going back to class and showing it off to the others!

But Matron was adamant, and said firmly, 'It won't do you any harm to have an extra day's rest, just to be on the safe side. As long as you don't have a relapse, you can join the others tomorrow.'

Esme had a steady stream of visitors throughout the day. Miss Grayling popped in, which made Esme feel very honoured indeed. And most of the third formers came to see her, as they thought that she had done a rather noble thing, and were secretly quite impressed.

Bonnie and Amy, armed with a large bottle of barley-sugar, visited after breakfast. Pam and Nora spent their lunch break gathering a huge bunch of the most beautiful wild flowers, which they presented to the invalid. And Felicity and Susan went along to the San after tea, taking a book for Esme to read, in case she was bored. Esme's ordeal had taken it out of her more than she realised and, despite her protestations that she felt well enough to return to class, she was beginning to feel a little tired. Felicity, who had intended to give the girl a scold for putting herself in danger, relented when she saw the large bruise on Esme's head, and noticed how pale she looked. Instead she said, 'Poor old thing! You have had a bad time of it, haven't you? Never mind, I daresay Matron will soon have you back to your old self.'

The two girls hadn't been there long when Matron herself bustled in, saying, 'It's time for Esme to have her nap now, girls. Please tell the others that she is to have no more visitors today.'

'What a tyrant you are, Matron!' complained Susan, as they were shooed out.

'I need to be a tyrant to keep you girls in order!' said Matron. But there was a smile on her face, and Felicity and Susan laughed as they went off to join the others.

They were all lazing about on the grass before prep, and Pam said, 'Isn't it a simply glorious day? I wish that we could do our prep out here.'

'If Miss Peters was taking us she might agree to it,' said Freddie. 'But it's Mam'zelle Dupont, and you know how she hates being outdoors for too long in the hot weather.'

'Yes, she's simply terrified of wasps,' laughed Felicity. 'And she can't bear all the flies buzzing around.'

'I bet I could get her to agree to it,' said June, who had been looking thoughtful. She jumped to her feet suddenly and said, 'Nora, come with me!'

'Why?' asked Nora, looking quite startled. She was stretched out on the grass with her hands behind her head, and looked very comfortable indeed. 'I'd just as soon stay here, if it's all the same to you.'

'Do you want to do your prep in a stuffy classroom, or would you rather do it out here?' demanded June.

Nora sighed, and sat up. 'I don't suppose I shall get any peace unless I agree to go with you. Where are we going, by the way?'

'To find Mam'zelle, of course,' said June, with a grin. 'Come on!'

The two girls walked off towards the school together, June talking rapidly to Nora as they went. They found Mam'zelle in the mistresses' common-room, where she was marking the fifth form's French essays. At least, that was what she was *supposed* to be doing, but it was so hot that she simply couldn't concentrate. She had taken off her high-heeled shoes and undone the collar of her blouse, and was fanning herself with one of the fifth formers' work.

Nora stifled a giggle as she peeped at the mistress through the open door, and June frowned at her, pulling her back along the corridor. Loudly she said, 'Mam'zelle Dupont would never agree to such a thing, Nora! Now, if it was Mam'zelle Rougier . . .'

'Nonsense!' replied Nora, just as loudly. 'Why, Mam'zelle Dupont is *far* more good-hearted than Mam'zelle Rougier – and a much better teacher. She knows that we can't possibly do our best work if we feel hot and uncomfortable.'

Mam'zelle stopped fanning herself abruptly as she heard the voices, recognising them at once. It was the bad June, and dear Nora – ah, what a good girl she was, to speak so kindly of her old Mam'zelle. The French mistress smiled to herself as she heard June say, 'I quite agree that Mam'zelle Dupont is an excellent teacher. In fact, I would go so far as to say that she is the best in the entire school. But I still say that she would never allow us to do our prep out in the open air.' June gave rather a scornful laugh, and added, 'She's far too scared of wasps and things.'

'What rubbish you do talk, June!' scoffed Nora. 'Mam'zelle might be scared of wasps, but she has pluck, and I know that she would brush her fear aside for the good of us girls.'

'Very well, then,' said June. 'If you're so convinced, you go and find Mam'zelle, and ask her if we can take our prep outside. I bet she's in our classroom right now, getting our work ready, for she always takes such care over our lessons.'

Nora sighed and said sorrowfully, 'I can't, June. You see, I wouldn't feel right taking advantage of Mam'zelle's good nature.'

'She is *very* good-natured, isn't she?' agreed June. 'If only some of the other mistresses were more like her! Though I still say that she would never consider letting us do our prep out of doors.' Then she sighed. 'Ah well, I suppose we shall just have to resign ourselves to a hot, uncomfortable hour in our stuffy old classroom.'

Then the two girls moved away, their voices fading into the distance as they walked down the corridor. Mam'zelle, meanwhile, sat completely still, feeling quite moved by all she had heard. Ah, the dear girls! They might play tricks on her sometimes, but they were fond of their old Mam'zelle. The best teacher in the school! Good-natured and good-hearted! Mam'zelle's heart felt warm as she remembered the girls' remarks. And Nora had said that she had the pluck. Mam'zelle knew what a great compliment that was, for English girls set great store by pluck! They were good girls, these third formers, and they deserved a treat. And she, Mam'zelle Dupont, would give them one. Ah yes, she would prove to them that everything they had said about her was true.

So, when the third formers trooped rather dispiritedly into their classroom for prep that afternoon, they were in for a surprise. Mam'zelle was already at her desk, and her little black eyes danced as she looked at the girls' weary, slumped shoulders and dragging feet.

'Freddie!' she cried, making her voice very stern. 'Stand up straight, and do not slouch so!'

'But Mam'zelle, it's so hot!' groaned Freddie.

'That is not an excuse for laziness,' snapped Mam'zelle. 'I expect you all to work hard at your prep tonight, no matter how hot you feel.'

'Yes, Mam'zelle,' everyone groaned.

'Good!' Then Mam'zelle's face broke into a broad grin and she said, 'Pick up your books, everyone, and follow me. For tonight, we do our prep outside!'

The girls looked at one another in amazement, then a resounding cheer broke out!

'Hurrah! What fun!'

'Yes, we'll work twice as hard out in the fresh air.'

'You're a real sport, Mam'zelle!'

As Mam'zelle beamed round, June nudged Nora and whispered, 'See! I told you it would work.'

Only Amy and Bonnie were not pleased at being allowed to do their prep outside, for neither of them were outdoor types. Also, both were terrified of getting freckles, and Bonnie pleaded with Mam'zelle.

'Can't Amy and I do our work in the classroom, Mam'zelle?' she asked in her soft voice, making her eyes as big as possible. 'We won't play the fool, I promise you.'

'I know that you will not, *ma chère*,' said Mam'zelle, patting the girl's cheek fondly. 'But, alas, it is the rule that you must be supervised whilst working at your prep. But do not worry, for you and Amy and I shall sit in the shade of one of the big trees, then none of us shall catch a freckle!'

So out they all went, and the third formers were true to their word, working most conscientiously. It was a pleasant late afternoon, for a cooling, gentle breeze sprang up, which was very refreshing, and Mam'zelle congratulated herself on making a good decision. Even when a caterpillar crawled on to the toe of her shoe, the French mistress was not unduly disturbed. She gave a little start when she first spotted it, but then she remembered Nora's remark earlier – she would prove that she had the pluck! But Mam'zelle could not bring herself to remove it, instead asking Bonnie, who was sitting beside her, to do it. Bonnie didn't care for what she called 'creepy-crawlies' any more than Mam'zelle did, so she picked up a twig and managed to dislodge it with that, earning the French mistress's undying gratitude. Nothing else occurred to mar the afternoon, and when the third formers gathered in the common-room after prep, they were in good spirits.

'Wasn't it fun having prep out of doors?' said Susan. 'A super end to the day.'

'It's been a funny sort of day, with poor old Esme laid up in the San,' said Nora.

'It's been a funny sort of *term*, if you ask me,' said Pam. 'What with Bill and Clarissa's troubles, and Lucy and Esme feuding.'

'Yes, but I believe that things are coming right,' said Felicity, who had been looking thoughtful. 'Lucy and Esme are friends again, and things seem to have gone quiet over at Five Oaks. It looks as if all our problems are behind us, and the second half of the term will be nice and peaceful.'

But Felicity had spoken too soon. For the third formers were in for a very big shock indeed!

A shock for Julie

The next morning, Felicity and Susan were making their way downstairs to breakfast, a little way ahead of the others, when they saw a boyish figure striding across the hall.

'I say, isn't that Bill?' said Susan.

'I believe it is,' said Felicity, calling out, 'Hi, Bill!'

But Bill was either in a great hurry or she simply didn't hear Felicity, for she carried on her way without so much as glancing up, and soon disappeared from view.

'Was that Bill I just spotted?' asked June, coming down the stairs behind the two girls. 'I wonder what she's doing at Malory Towers? And at such an early hour in the morning, too.'

'Perhaps she's come to visit Miss Peters,' suggested Susan.

'Before breakfast?' said Felicity. 'I doubt it. She seemed in an awful rush, wherever she was going.'

Miss Peters was already in the dining-room, having her breakfast, when the third formers entered, so it seemed that Bill had not come to Malory Towers to see her, after all. And someone else was already there, too – Esme! The third formers cheered when they saw her seated at their table and, in the excitement of greeting her, soon forgot about Bill.

'How are you feeling, Esme, old girl?'

'Good to have you back!'

'My word, that's a simply splendid bruise you have there!'

'You should part your hair on the side,' said Amy, looking at her critically. 'Then it will cover the bruise.'

'What a good idea!' exclaimed Esme. 'I think I shall wait until morning school has finished, though.' Lowering her voice, she added, 'Dear old Mam'zelle Dupont has been fussing over me like anything, thanks to my bruise. Perhaps it will work on Miss Peters too, and she will go a bit easy on me in class this morning.'

Esme did look much better today, though, thought Felicity. The colour had come back to her cheeks and, judging by the way she was tucking into her porridge, her appetite had returned too. Lucy, of course, was thrilled to have her cousin back. They might never be best friends again, but what had happened yesterday had created a bond between them. And Lucy sincerely hoped that that bond would never be broken.

Breakfast was nearly over when one of the school maids came into the dining-room and went across to Miss Peters. The maid said something to her in a low voice, and Miss Peters nodded, a slight frown on her heavy face, and got to her feet. Then she came over to the third formers and said, 'Julie! Miss Grayling wants me to take you to her study at once.'

Julie looked most alarmed, and began wracking her brains. But she couldn't think of a single reason why the Head would want to see her.

'Do you know what she wants, Miss Peters?' she asked, rather apprehensively.

Miss Peters shook her head, and said, 'I have no idea. But we had better not keep her waiting.'

'Heavens!' exclaimed Nora, her blue eyes wide, and her fluffy blonde hair looking almost as if it was standing on end. 'I do hope that Julie isn't in trouble. Has she been up to mischief, Lucy?'

Lucy, puzzled and a little worried, shook her head, while Pam said soberly, 'I say! I do hope that it isn't bad news from home.'

'Oh, don't say that, Pam!' pleaded Felicity. 'That would be just too awful.'

But Julie had still not returned by the time the girls made their way to their first lesson. And nor had Miss Peters, who was supposed to be taking the class.

Five minutes went by, then another five, and at last June said, 'Well, it doesn't look as if we're going to have our Geography lesson this morning at all!'

Normally the girls would have been delighted at this, but now they all felt rather uneasy. At the moment, each and every one of them would have given anything to see Miss Peters stride in, along with Julie.

'I wish we knew what was happening,' said Felicity fretfully.

'It must be something very serious for Miss Grayling to keep her so long,' said Susan, a grave expression on her face.

'But why is Miss Peters there too?' asked Lucy. 'I don't understand.'

No one understood, and just then Nora, who sat by the window, exclaimed, 'I say, who's this? Why, it's Clarissa!'

At once all the third formers dashed to the window, to see Clarissa walking up the drive. She looked awfully serious as she made her way to the big front door, and Susan said, 'Do you suppose that Clarissa is going to see Miss Grayling, too? And is that where Bill has disappeared to?'

'The plot thickens!' said June. 'I've a good mind to sneak along to the Head's study and put my ear to the door.'

'June, no!' said Felicity, firmly. 'If you were caught you would get into a fearful row, and the last thing we need is more trouble.'

June looked as if she was about to argue, but just then Bonnie squealed, 'Look! A police car!'

Everyone gasped, for now a police car was making its way up the drive, and the girls watched, open-mouthed, as a very serious-looking policeman got out.

The third formers looked at one another in consternation, and, with a rather nervous laugh, Freddie said, 'Heavens! Has Julie robbed a bank, or something?'

The girls watched and waited, and, at last, Bill and Clarissa emerged, so deep in conversation that they didn't even notice the third formers at the window.

'What a lot of coming and going!' said Freddie. 'But we are still no nearer to finding out what has happened.'

The time passed very slowly, as the girls waited for news. Then, at last, a few minutes before the lesson was due to end, Miss Potts came into the room, a very worried look on her face.

'Girls, Miss Peters will not be able to return to class before the end of the lesson,' she said, looking at the anxious faces before her. 'You may all go to break a few minutes earlier than usual.'

But even this news could not cheer up the third formers, and Lucy asked fearfully, 'Please, Miss Potts, do you know where Julie is? We're all terribly worried about her.'

'She has just gone along to the common-room,' answered Miss Potts heavily. 'Please be very kind to her when you see her, for I am afraid that she has had some extremely bad news.'

With that, Miss Potts left the room and, at once, a perfect babble broke out.

'Something has happened at home. I knew it!'

'It's Jack! Something has happened to Jack. Perhaps he's sick.'

'Oh yes, people always call the police when they have a sick horse on their hands!' said June sarcastically.

'I must go to her,' said Felicity, getting to her feet. 'She may be in need of comfort, or someone to talk to.'

'Felicity!' said Lucy, suddenly. 'May I go, instead of you? I know that you are head of the form, but I am Julie's best friend.'

Felicity thought for a moment, and then said decidedly, 'We shall all go! Then Julie will know that she has the whole form behind her, and that – whatever has happened – we shall all do what we can to help.'

So every one of the third formers, even spoilt, selfish

Amy, trooped to the common-room, where they found Julie sitting alone on a settee. She looked up as the door opened, her expression so bleak that the girls felt frightened. Her eyes were red, and it was obvious that she had been crying. But Julie *never* cried! At once, Felicity and Lucy rushed to sit either side of her, Felicity putting a comforting arm about her shoulders as she said gently, 'What is it, Julie, old girl?'

'It's Jack,' answered Julie, her voice sounding unnaturally high. 'He's gone. He's been stolen from Five Oaks.'

A horrified gasp went round the room. So *that* was why Bill and Clarissa had been here! And that was the reason the police had been called.

'Do the police have any clues?' asked June.

'Not really,' answered Julie, stifling a sob. 'There were faint tyre tracks in the lane leading to Five Oaks, so he may have been taken away in a horse box. But there is nothing to tell them who the thief is.'

'I can't believe that Bill and Clarissa would be so careless!' said Susan, shocked. 'After everything that has happened, I should have thought that they would be on their guard. But to let someone simply walk away with Jack, right under their noses –'

'Oh, but it wasn't their fault,' broke in Julie. 'Truly it wasn't. For a start, Jack wasn't stolen in broad daylight. It happened last night, but the girls didn't discover that he was gone until this morning. And the thief created a diversion.'

'A diversion? What do you mean, Julie?' asked Pam.

'You see, someone started a fire in the field behind the house, late last night,' explained Julie. 'It was right next to the small barn, where the girls store the hay for the horses. Bill said that it was only a small fire, but they were afraid that the barn would catch alight. So, of course, they had to dash out immediately and deal with it.'

'And, while they were putting the fire out, some wicked beast sneaked into the stable and took Jack,' finished Lucy, her eyes narrowed to slits. Angrily, she leapt up and began to pace the floor. 'My goodness, I hope that he's caught! I hope that the police lock him up and throw away the key! I hope –'

'Lucy, do calm down!' Felicity interrupted. 'And please stop pacing the floor like that, or you'll wear a hole in the carpet.'

'Sorry,' said Lucy, looking rather sheepish, as she stopped her pacing and sat down again. 'I just feel so terribly angry and upset!'

Lucy also felt a little guilty, too, because it could just as easily have been Sandy who was taken. But he was safe and well in his stall, while nobody knew where poor Jack was.

'Julie, have your people been told the news?' asked Nora.

'Yes, Miss Grayling telephoned them while I was in her study,' answered Julie. 'I was able to speak to them, too, and it was such a comfort. They both told me that they are certain Jack will come to no harm.'

'Of course he won't!' said Susan, bracingly. 'You may be sure that the police are doing everything possible to find him.'

'That's what Sergeant Dobbs told me,' said Julie. 'He's the policeman who came to see me this morning, and he was awfully nice. But I just feel so helpless! All I can do is wait, and wonder and worry!'

'Well, Julie, we will all be waiting, and wondering and worrying right beside you,' said Esme, who was quite as horrified as the others. What a welcome back this had turned out to be!

But the idea of sitting back and waiting for things to happen didn't appeal to June at all. She liked to be up and doing, and was turning over several ideas in her mind, which she prudently kept to herself, for Felicity most definitely would not approve.

Bonnie was also entertaining a pleasant daydream about unmasking the thief and reuniting Jack with his mistress. Why, if only she could pull it off she would be the heroine of the school!

The news of Jack's disappearance spread rapidly, of course, and everyone was shocked, for the little horse was a great character, and most of the girls loved him dearly. Several of the first formers were in tears, and had to be comforted by Matron and Mam'zelle Dupont. Not that tender-hearted Mam'zelle Dupont was much help, for she became so upset at the girls' distress that she had difficulty holding back her own tears!

Miss Peters, of course, understood better than any of the mistresses how Julie must be feeling, for she was a great horse lover. Her own beautiful horse, Midnight, meant more to her than anything, and she could only imagine how miserable she would feel if anything happened to him.

Even the stern Mam'zelle Rougier, who did not like horses at all, spoke kindly to Julie, and guarded her sharp tongue when the girl's thoughts wandered in class that afternoon.

Kay Foster, the Head Girl, came up to Julie, an earnest expression on her friendly, open face, as she said, 'What a dreadful thing to happen! Do let me know if there is any news, for everyone in the sixth form is terribly upset.'

Most surprisingly of all, Eleanor Banks sought Julie out and offered her sympathy. The third formers were in the courtyard when Eleanor – looking even paler than usual – approached them, and said to Julie, 'I'm so sorry to hear about what has happened. You must feel simply terrible.' Eleanor's voice shook a little as she went on, 'But I'm quite certain that you will have Jack back with you, safe and sound, in no time at all.'

Julie, rather taken aback at this, thanked Eleanor, but June, who had been watching the fifth former closely, raised her eyebrows and said, '*Why* are you so certain, Eleanor?'

But Eleanor immediately reverted to her usual, haughty manner, and said coldly, 'I was speaking to Julie, not to you, June.'

Then she stalked off, and Freddie said, 'Well! Wonders will never cease. Imagine the Ice Queen feeling sorry for someone!'

But Julie felt heartened by everyone's kindness and concern. That was one of the best things about a school like Malory Towers, she thought. When someone was in trouble, or things went wrong, everyone rallied round, ready to offer sympathy, and to help in any way they could. Even Eleanor Banks! Julie didn't much like the girl, but she desperately wanted to believe in her words. Jack would come back to her, safe and well. He *would*!

Detective work

June decided to pop over to Five Oaks and do a spot of investigating when afternoon lessons finished the following day and she was a little put out to discover that Bonnie had arrived a few minutes before her.

Each girl knew why the other was there, of course, and, after greeting one another, they went their separate ways.

June spoke to Clarissa, who looked very white and anxious.

'I feel absolutely terrible about Jack being stolen,' she told June. 'If the police don't find him, I don't know what I shall do.'

'It wasn't your fault, or Bill's,' said June. 'I don't see how either of you could have known that the fire was started to distract you.'

'Perhaps, but it doesn't stop us both from feeling guilty,' said Clarissa, sighing.

Just then, Bill came out of the house, and with her were two dark-haired, stocky young men.

'Who are they?' asked June curiously.

'Two of Bill's brothers,' said Clarissa. 'They are on leave from the army. Bill telephoned to tell them of our troubles. They said that they would come and stay for a while, to keep an eye on things.'

'Well, I should think that they will be more than capable of dealing with any intruders,' said June with a grin.

'Yes, and I must say that I do feel a great deal safer having Harry and John around,' said Clarissa. 'I just hope that it isn't too late to save Five Oaks.'

'Whatever do you mean?' asked June.

'Things aren't going well for us,' said Clarissa frankly. 'Of course, word has spread about Jack being stolen, and several people who had been stabling their horses with us have taken them away. And we aren't getting so many children coming for riding lessons as we used to. I suppose with Bill's accident, and then the fire, their parents feel that this isn't a very safe place.'

'But surely you're not thinking of selling Five Oaks?' said June, dismayed.

'We may have no choice,' said Clarissa, bleakly. 'You see, if we aren't making enough money, we simply can't afford to pay the bills or feed the horses. I know that Mr Banks would be happy to buy it from us, for he needs more room for his horses, and his land joins ours.'

'Is that so?' said June, narrowing her eyes thoughtfully. 'I say, Clarissa, would you mind if I have a scout round? I'd like to have a look at the place where the fire was started.'

'Be my guest,' said Clarissa. 'Though if you're looking for clues you won't find any, for the police have been over everything with a fine-tooth comb.'

Clarissa was right, for June found nothing that could be of any help at all.

Bonnie, however, *did* find something, though she was quite puzzled by it. The girl decided to take a look in the stable where Jack had been kept, in the hope that the thief might have been careless and dropped something. Eleanor Banks's beautiful white horse, Snowball, lived in the stall next-door-but-one to Jack's, and the fifth former was leading him out as Bonnie approached. Eleanor looked surprised and displeased to see Bonnie and said, 'What are you doing here?'

'I've come to see the horses,' answered Bonnie, coolly. 'Not that it's any business of yours, Eleanor.'

'Don't be cheeky!' said Eleanor, angrily. 'And if you have walked over here alone, it *is* my business. Girls from the lower forms are not allowed out on their own.'

This was true. The lower forms had to go out in twos or threes if they wanted to go into town, or take a walk along the cliffs. Normally everyone stuck to this rule very strictly – except when it came to visiting Bill and Clarissa. Because Five Oaks was only a few minutes' walk from Malory Towers, one or other of the girls would sometimes slip over alone. Most of the top formers turned a blind eye, but it was just like Eleanor to cause trouble! Thinking quickly, Bonnie said, 'Actually, June and I walked over together. She's here somewhere, and you can ask her if you don't believe me.'

She decided that she had better get hold of June later, and make sure that the two of them walked back to school together, just in case Eleanor was keeping an eye on them.

For now, though, the fifth former seemed satisfied, and

she walked away without another word, leaving Bonnie to pull a face behind her back.

Sandy, Lucy's pretty little horse, put his head over the door and whinnied a greeting. He was very pleased to see Bonnie, for he felt a little lonely now that his friend Jack was no longer living next door. Bonnie was a little nervous of some of the bigger horses, and was glad that they were all shut in, but Sandy was rather sweet, and very friendly. Bonnie patted his head and made a fuss of him, before going into the empty stable that had been Jack's, wrinkling her little nose up at the smell. Pooh! What on earth would Amy think if she could see her now?

Just then, something caught Bonnie's eye. A sheet of paper had been nailed to the wall.

Perhaps it's a ransom note, thought the girl excitedly, moving closer. But the sheet of paper was completely blank! How queer! Why on earth would someone nail a clean sheet of writing paper to the wall? Carefully removing it from the nail, Bonnie examined it closely. It couldn't have been there long, for it was clean and uncrumpled, with no signs of yellowing at all. Completely bewildered, the girl folded the paper up and put it in the pocket of her dress. It wasn't much of a clue, but it was all that she had!

Shortly afterwards, Bonnie went off to find June. She told the girl about her encounter with Eleanor and said, 'If she catches either of us walking back alone, I bet her punishment will be to confine us to the grounds, or something beastly like that.'

'Yes, that would be just like Eleanor,' said June scornfully. 'Well, I'm ready to go back to school, if you are.'

As the two girls walked along the lane to Malory Towers, Bonnie asked, 'Did you find anything useful?'

'Not a thing,' said June in disgust. 'You?'

'Well, I didn't find anything useful, but I did find something rather peculiar,' said Bonnie, and she pulled the piece of blank paper from her pocket. 'This was nailed to the wall of Jack's stable.'

'How odd!' said June, taking the paper and scrutinising it carefully, as Bonnie had done earlier. 'Why on earth would someone want to nail a perfectly plain piece of paper to the stable wall?'

'I simply can't imagine,' said Bonnie, folding the paper up again and putting it back in her pocket. 'I got quite excited when I spotted it, thinking that it might be a ransom note, but it turned out to be nothing of the sort.'

Then she sighed and said, 'I was talking to Bill earlier. Things are looking pretty black for her and Clarissa. They may have to sell Five Oaks.'

'Yes, Clarissa was telling me the same thing,' said June. She was silent and thoughtful for a moment, then she said in a rush, 'You know, Bonnie, I wanted to be the one to find Jack, and unmask the person who was behind all these beastly tricks simply for my own glory, and so that I could bask in everyone's admiration. I think that you had the same idea, didn't you?'

'Yes,' admitted Bonnie rather solemnly. 'But, since talking to Bill, I don't feel like that any more. It doesn't matter *who* solves the mystery. What is important is that *someone* solves it – and quickly! The girls' livelihood is at stake, and Julie needs to be reunited with Jack as quickly as possible.'

'That's exactly how I feel now,' said June. 'Perhaps we would get further if we worked as a team.'

'You and me?' said Bonnie, sounding very surprised.

'Yes, why not?' said June. 'Two heads are better than one, and all that.'

'All right, then,' agreed Bonnie. 'We'll pool our resources. Not that there's anything to pool at the moment!'

The other third formers had been very busy too. Felicity had come up with the idea of making some notices about the missing horse, and sticking them up around town.

'You know the kind of thing,' she said. 'We could write a description of Jack, and I'm sure that Miss Grayling won't mind if we put the telephone number of the school on them.'

'Yes, then we can stick them on lamp posts and trees, and ask some of the shopkeepers in town if they wouldn't mind putting them in their windows,' said Susan.

'That's a marvellous idea!' Julie said. 'It would make me feel as if I was actually doing something to help find Jack.'

'What a pity we can't offer a reward,' said Susan. 'I'm sure that would encourage people to go and look for him.'

'Perhaps we can,' said Julie. 'I'm sure that my father would put up some money, though it won't be an awful lot. And I would give up my pocket money for a year if it meant getting Jack back.'

'Let's get to work on the notices now,' said Pam. 'And then we can go out after lunch tomorrow and put them up.'

Miss Linnie, the art mistress, was happy to provide the girls with some paper, and allowed them to use the art-room to work on their notices.

'We can do the writing in bright colours, so that it will be really eye-catching,' said Felicity. 'And perhaps we can use some of Miss Linnie's special coloured paper for some of them.'

Pam, who was very good at art, did a beautiful and very life-like drawing of Jack on her notice, and coloured it in carefully.

'Pam, that's Jack to the life!' exclaimed Esme in admiration.

'Yes, you've even put in the little white patch that he has over one eye,' said Julie. 'We must put your notice in the sweet-shop, for that always seems to be busy, and lots of people will see it.'

Even Amy, who generally had little time to spare for anyone's worries but her own, made one of the 'missing' notices.

'It's good to know that she's willing to do her bit when someone is in trouble,' said Felicity to Susan as they went in to tea.

'Yes – though I expect she only joined us because Bonnie wasn't about, and she was at a bit of a loose end,' said Susan.

'Where *is* Bonnie?' asked Felicity. 'I haven't seen her

for simply ages. Or June either, for that matter.'

The two girls were at the tea table when the third formers went into the dining-room, hungrily tucking into bread and butter.

'We've been over to Five Oaks,' said June, and began to tell the others the news that Bill and Clarissa might have to sell up.

'They can't!' cried a horrified Nora. 'Why, Malory Towers just wouldn't be the same without Bill and Clarissa just along the road.'

'Isn't there *something* we can do to help?' asked Lucy.

'The only thing that will help is finding Jack, and the person who is trying to ruin the girls' business,' said Bonnie. 'And I'm afraid we seem to have come to a bit of a dead end there.'

But something was niggling away at the back of June's mind. Something concerning that piece of paper Bonnie had found. There was something significant about it, she was sure – if only she could think what!

The answer came to her in a flash, as she was in the common-room that evening. June suddenly sat bolt upright in her chair, and looked around for Bonnie. The girl was nowhere to be seen, and June called out, 'Amy! Where is Bonnie?'

'She's gone to fetch something from the dorm,' said Amy, and, in an instant, June was out of the door.

'Bonnie!' she cried, bursting into the dormitory. 'Where is that piece of paper that you found in Jack's stable? Oh, don't say that you've thrown it away!'

'Of course not,' said Bonnie, producing it from her pocket. 'What do you want with it, June?'

'I think that there might be something written on it after all,' June said. 'Do you remember, a few weeks ago, I slipped a bottle of invisible ink into Eleanor's bag?'

'Yes, I remember,' said Bonnie. 'Golly! Do you think that Eleanor might have written something on here, not realising that she was using invisible ink?'

'It's possible,' said June. 'It takes about ten minutes for the writing to disappear, so if Eleanor nailed the note up immediately after she had written it, she wouldn't know that no one would be able to read it.'

'Yes, but what reason could Eleanor possibly have for writing a note and putting it on the wall of Jack's stable?' said Bonnie, frowning. 'I say, June! You surely don't think that she could be behind Jack's disappearance, and all the horrible things that have happened to Bill and Clarissa?'

'I think that her uncle could,' answered June, gravely. 'And I think that Eleanor could be helping him. You see, Clarissa told me that Mr Banks would like to buy Five Oaks. So perhaps he is trying to drive the girls out.'

'I believe that you could be right!' said Bonnie excitedly. 'But what a pity that we can't read what was written on that paper.'

'We can,' said June, grinning. 'If we make the room dark, and shine a torch on the paper, we should be able to make out the writing. Draw the curtains, Bonnie!'

Swiftly, Bonnie darted to the big windows at the end of the dormitory and pulled the curtains across, while June fetched a torch from her locker. Then the two girls sat side by side on Bonnie's bed, and June shone the torch on the piece of paper.

The girls could hardly breathe as writing appeared, very faint, but readable.

'To Bill and Clarissa,' June read aloud. 'If you want Jack back, follow these instructions exactly. Both of you must come to the clearing in Bluebell Wood at midnight tonight. Don't tell the police, and don't inform anyone else of the contents of this note.'

The two girls stared at one another in consternation.

'Midnight tonight,' gasped Bonnie. 'June, what are we to do? Should we take the note to Miss Grayling? Someone must tell Bill and Clarissa! And Julie ought to be told, too.'

'Hush a minute,' said June, getting to her feet. 'I need to think!'

There was silence for a few moments, then at last June said, 'We can't take the note to Miss Grayling, for she is out. She and Miss Potts are going to the theatre tonight. And we can't tell Julie, in case this turns out to be a hoax, or something goes wrong. She would have her hopes raised, only for them to be dashed again.'

'Yes, that's true,' said Bonnie. 'June, do you think we should telephone the police?'

'Absolutely not!' said June, firmly. 'You saw what the note said, Bonnie. I think that we should sneak into the Head's study, and telephone Bill and Clarissa.'

'All right,' said Bonnie, standing up. 'Let's be quick then. You can telephone, and I'll keep watch.'

So the two girls sped downstairs and made their way to

Miss Grayling's study. Fortunately they didn't meet any mistresses on the way, but both of them felt very nervous as they opened the door to the Head's neat, comfortable study. June walked over to the desk and lifted the telephone receiver, while Bonnie stood at the door, looking up and down the corridor. At last, Bill answered the telephone and June poured out her story. The conversation seemed to take simply ages, for, of course, the astonished Bill had a great many questions to ask. But it was finally over and the two girls left Miss Grayling's study, shutting the door behind them.

'What did Bill say?' asked Bonnie. 'Are she and Clarissa going to the wood?'

'Yes,' answered June. 'But Bill's brothers are going to go there about half an hour before them, and lie in wait. What a jolly good thing that they turned up today!'

'Where is Bluebell Wood, anyway?' asked Bonnie.

'About a mile down the road from Five Oaks,' said June. 'We sometimes have picnics there. It's a beautiful spot during the day, but I should imagine that it's a little creepy at night.'

Bonnie gave a shudder. 'I wonder who will be there to meet Bill and Clarissa?' she said. 'Eleanor, or her uncle?'

'I shouldn't imagine that it will be either of them,' said June. 'Neither of them will want to come out into the open and admit that they are involved. It will probably be one of Mr Banks's grooms, or someone else that he has paid to do his dirty work for him!'

'Well, whoever he is, he's in for quite a shock when

he runs into Bill's brothers,' said Bonnie with grim satisfaction. 'They will make him talk, all right, then the game will be up for Mr Banks!'

'Yes,' said June, with a broad grin. 'And I intend to be there to see it!'

'June!' gasped Bonnie. 'You can't sneak out of the school at midnight!'

'Oh no,' said June blithely. 'I shall have to leave much earlier than that, if I'm to get a good seat. There's a nice big apple tree in the wood. I think I shall climb up there to watch. No one will be able to see me, but I shall have a splendid view!'

'You'll get into the most frightful row if you're caught!' said Bonnie, quite horrified.

'Well, I shan't be,' said June confidently. 'I shall slip out of the side door that leads into the garden, and leave it unlocked so that I can sneak back in again. And I'll borrow a bicycle from the shed, so that I can get there and back quickly. No one will be any the wiser – except you, of course, and I know that you won't say anything!'

'I shan't, of course, but I do wish that you would change your mind, June,' said Bonnie, looking rather unhappy. She couldn't think of anything more frightening than being alone in the wood at midnight, and simply couldn't understand why June was willing to risk a terrible punishment to be there.

'I won't change my mind,' said June. 'I wouldn't miss this for the world!'

A thrilling night

June didn't dare let herself fall asleep, in case she didn't wake up in time to join the fray at Bluebell Wood. She couldn't set her alarm clock, of course, in case the others heard it. Felicity would have a fit if she knew what June meant to do!

Bonnie was awake, too. Not from choice, but because she felt so uneasy about June's plan that she simply couldn't sleep.

The others, however, slept soundly, and when eleven o'clock struck, only Bonnie saw June slip from her bed and quietly get dressed. Then the girl put her bolster and pillow down the middle of the bed, pulling the covers over so that it looked as if someone was asleep there. If Miss Peters should happen to look in, that would fool her nicely!

June almost jumped out of her skin when Bonnie whispered her name as she walked past her bed.

'What is it?' June whispered back.

'Do be careful!' said Bonnie in a low voice. 'I shan't be able to sleep until I know that you're back safely.'

'Don't worry about me,' said June, smiling into the darkness. 'I shall have a fine night's entertainment and I'll be back before you know it!'

Miss Peters did look in, about ten minutes after June had left, but she didn't put the light on and went away again quickly, quite satisfied that nothing was amiss. After she had gone, Bonnie decided that it was pointless even trying to sleep, and sat up in bed, hugging her knees. Perhaps she should borrow June's torch, then she could read her book under the covers. But June had probably taken it with her. What a shame, for a diversion was just what Bonnie needed, to take her mind off things.

A diversion! The word seemed to trigger something in Bonnie's head, and suddenly she turned pale, as a thought occurred to her. A shocking, horrible thought! She sprang out of bed and went to Felicity, shaking her.

'Felicity!' she hissed in her ear. 'Felicity, do wake up!'

Startled, Felicity opened her eyes and sat up sharply.

'Bonnie!' she whispered, none too pleased. 'What on earth do you mean by waking me like this?'

'I need to talk to you,' murmured Bonnie urgently. 'Come into the bathroom, so that we don't wake the others.'

Tired, cross and bewildered, Felicity got out of bed, and reluctantly followed Bonnie into the bathroom at the end of the dormitory.

'What is it, Bonnie?' asked Felicity with a yawn, as she shut the bathroom door behind her.

As quickly as she could, Bonnie told Felicity of how she and June had discovered the note to Clarissa and Bill, of how they had alerted the two girls and, finally, of how June had gone off alone to Bluebell Wood, to watch the drama unfold. Wide awake now, Felicity listened open-mouthed. 'You and June have done very well,' she said at last. 'But what an idiot June is, to sneak off to the woods like that! It's bad enough being caught out of bed at night, but if she's caught outside the school she could be expelled! Just wait until I see her!'

'Yes, but do listen, Felicity!' said Bonnie, impatiently. 'On the night Jack was stolen, someone started a fire behind the house to create a diversion, remember?'

'Of course I remember,' said Felicity. 'But I really don't –'

'Don't you see?' cried Bonnie. 'Suppose that this note to Bill and Clarissa is a diversion too? To get them away from Five Oaks, so that Mr Banks – if he *is* the one who is behind all this – can do something else? Why, he might be planning on setting fire to the house, or stealing the rest of the horses, or – or anything!'

'My goodness!' gasped Felicity, pressing her hands to her cheeks. 'You could be right! And, if you *are* right, we must telephone the police at once. There's not a moment to lose!'

So, for the second time that evening, Bonnie found herself on the way to Miss Grayling's study to use the telephone.

She came to a halt outside the door and turned to Felicity, whispering, 'Suppose that the Head is in there? She must be back from the theatre by now.'

'Yes, but surely she will have gone to bed,' said Felicity. 'Besides, the chances are that we will have to wake her and tell her what has happened anyway! I shouldn't be at all surprised if the police turn up here, once they have finished at Five Oaks.'

So Bonnie tapped timidly at the door, but the Head's voice did not call out, so she pushed it open and went in. This time Felicity kept a look-out, while Bonnie called the police. Then she telephoned Five Oaks, to see if she could warn Bill and Clarissa of her suspicions, but there was no reply.

'They must have left for Bluebell Wood already,' said Bonnie. 'But the policeman that I spoke to said that he is going to send someone over to Five Oaks at once.'

'It's ten minutes to midnight,' said Felicity, coming further into the room and glancing at the clock on the wall. 'If Mr Banks is planning something, he won't act until midnight, when he knows that Bill and Clarissa will be out of the way.'

'Do you think that we ought to go and wake Miss Grayling, or Miss Peters?' asked Bonnie. 'I'd really rather not, but if you think that the police will turn up, perhaps we had better.'

And then the two girls got the shock of their lives, for a familiar voice spoke behind them.

'There is no need to wake me, girls,' it said. 'For I am already awake.'

Felicity and Bonnie had been standing with their backs to the door, and they turned sharply to see Miss Grayling standing there, in her dressing-gown.

'I thought that I heard a noise, and came to investigate,' she said, looking rather stern. 'I trust that the two of you have a good explanation for being in my study at this hour.'

'We do, Miss Grayling,' said Felicity, realising that there was nothing for it but to tell the Head everything now. Though she would try to keep the fact that June had sneaked away from the school out of it, of course!

Miss Grayling went and sat behind her desk, indicating that the two girls should sit opposite her. Bonnie had grown quite tired of recounting the events of the evening, so she let Felicity do the talking, interpolating a word here and there.

The Head was very shocked, of course, particularly when the name of Eleanor Banks was mentioned.

'If it is proved that Eleanor has been involved in this terrible business, her future at Malory Towers will be in serious doubt,' said Miss Grayling very gravely.

'Well, if it hadn't been for that note, written in invisible ink, we wouldn't have suspected that she, and her uncle, were involved at all,' said Bonnie.

Miss Grayling smiled, and said, 'You and June are to be congratulated, Bonnie. That was a very neat piece of detective work. Where *is* June, by the way?'

Felicity hesitated for a moment, not quite liking to lie to the Head. Bonnie, however, had no such scruples, and said at once, 'Why, asleep in bed, of course, Miss Grayling.'

'It's not like June to be asleep when there's excitement afoot,' said Miss Grayling, raising her eyebrows. 'Didn't you think to wake her, Bonnie, when you realised that the note might have been a ruse to get Bill and Clarissa out of the way?'

'No, for she seemed so tired earlier,' said Bonnie, glibly. 'And I thought that Felicity was the proper person to consult, as she is head of the form.'

'Well, you both acted very sensibly in calling the police,' said the Head. 'Of course, you should have come to me first, or to Miss Potts, but I realise that time was of the essence.'

Then she noticed that Felicity was shivering slightly. Both girls had come downstairs without their dressing-gowns on, and although the days were hot, the nights were a little chilly.

'Let me go and find Matron,' said Miss Grayling, getting to her feet. 'I'll ask her to make us all some nice, hot cocoa.'

'Phew, that was close!' said Felicity, as the door closed behind the Head. 'For a moment, I was afraid that Miss Grayling was going to suggest that we wake June.'

'So was I,' said Bonnie, with a nervous giggle. 'I do hope that she comes back soon, and manages to get in without being seen!'

Soon Miss Grayling was back, followed by Matron, bearing a tray with three mugs of steaming cocoa on it.

'Well!' said Matron, putting the tray on the desk. 'Miss Grayling tells me that you girls have had quite an adventure this evening. Now, you drink this cocoa and it will warm you up. I don't know what you're thinking of, wandering around without your dressing-gowns on.'

The two girls hoped fervently that Matron wouldn't

take it into her head to go up to the dormitory and fetch their dressing-gowns herself. Her sharp eyes would soon spot that June's bed was empty if she did that!

Luckily, though, it seemed that Matron was far too busy, for she said, 'I must dash, for I have young Jenny from the second form in bed with a stomach upset, and I don't want to leave her for too long.'

Heaving a sigh of relief, Felicity and Bonnie sipped their cocoa, and hoped that June would not be long. Both girls were beginning to feel most peculiar. They felt very tired, but at the same time very excited. And there was more excitement to come, for as the girls drank the last of their cocoa, they heard the sound of cars outside. Miss Grayling went to the window and pulled aside the curtain.

'The police are here,' she said, turning back to the girls. 'Now, perhaps, we shall find out if this mysterious note really was a ruse, after all. And no doubt they will want to interview you, Bonnie, and June.'

Felicity and Bonnie exchanged glances of horror, and the Head said, 'I hate to disturb June, but I really think that you had better go and fetch her, Bonnie.'

June, meanwhile, was not enjoying herself at all. She had borrowed a bicycle from the shed and ridden to Blueberry Wood, hiding it in a hedge before shinning up the big apple tree. Then she had settled herself as comfortably as possible on a large branch, her back against the trunk, and waited for events to unfold. Bill's brothers had arrived a few moments later, and June watched as the two of them hid in the bushes, snatches of their conversation floating up to her on the still night air.

'I hope this fellow isn't going to keep us waiting for too long,' said John, in a menacing tone. 'I've a thing or two that I want to say to him!'

'Yes, he might be a little more careful about who he picks on next, when we've finished with him,' growled Harry.

'We'd better keep quiet now,' said John. 'If we frighten him off before the girls turn up, the whole thing will have been a waste of time.'

Then, a little later, Bill and Clarissa themselves turned up on horseback, both of them looking pale and nervous.

The two girls caught a glimpse of John and Harry in their hiding place, but ignored them, in case anyone else was watching.

However, the only person watching was June, and she soon grew heartily bored. There was no sign of anyoneelse, no sound of footsteps, no snapping of twigs. She was also becoming very uncomfortable, perched on her branch, with the trunk of the tree digging into her back. The minutes ticked by, and the people in the wood heard the sound of a car in the distance. Everyone waited with bated breath, but the sound died away, and all was silent again.

'Well!' said Bill, at last. 'It doesn't look as if anyone is coming, does it?'

'No,' agreed Clarissa, sounding rather crestfallen. 'Blow! I really did hope that we would have some good news for Julie tomorrow.'

The two boys came out from the bushes and dusted themselves down.

'Might as well go home,' June heard Harry saying. 'Either that note that the girls found was a hoax, or the writer has got cold feet.'

And with that, the four of them departed, and a very disgruntled June climbed down from the tree. What a waste of a perfectly good night! To think that she could have been tucked up in her cosy bed, instead of sitting up a tree! And, worst of all, Jack was still missing. Thank goodness that they hadn't let Julie in on the secret, and built her hopes up, for her disappointment would have been hard to bear.

The thought of her bed was a very welcome one indeed, and June yawned as she mounted her bicycle. Soon she was cycling along the lane towards Malory Towers, but, alas, with the school in sight, she came to grief. A rabbit darted across the lane in front of her, and June swerved to avoid it, falling off the bicycle and landing in an undignified heap. June was more shocked than hurt – or so she thought, until she tried to stand up and discovered that she had painfully twisted her ankle. With a little groan of pain, she righted the bicycle and gingerly climbed back on. But it was far more painful to pedal than to walk, so, clinging to the handlebars for support, the girl hobbled the last few yards to the school, and through the gates. And then what a shock she got! Two police cars were parked on the drive, and lights were blazing all over the school. What *was* going on?

Heroines and villains

June looked at the scene before her open-mouthed. Well, really! She had spent the last hour or so waiting for something to happen, and it seemed that all the excitement had been taking place at Malory Towers! Now, if only she could get back in without being spotted.

Her ankle was growing more painful now, and June limped slowly across to the shed, where she replaced the bicycle. Then, keeping close to the bushes, she made her way to the little side door, which she had left unlocked. As she was about to turn the handle, the door was suddenly pulled open, and June almost fell inside, very relieved to see that the person standing there wasn't Miss Grayling, or Miss Potts – but Bonnie! And the girl was holding June's pyjamas and dressing-gown.

'Thank heavens,' said Bonnie, thrusting the clothes at June. 'Get changed, quickly! Miss Grayling has sent me to fetch you.'

'Miss Grayling wants to see me? Why? Bonnie, do tell me what's happened!' begged June. 'There are police cars in the drive, and lights on all over the place, and –'

'Never mind that now!' said Bonnie, impatiently. 'Get into your pyjamas, for I've been gone simply ages, and the

Head will send someone to look for me if I don't take you to her soon. I'll explain everything to you on the way.'

So June scrambled into her pyjamas, and Bonnie threw her day clothes into a nearby cupboard, saying, 'We can collect these later. Now, make your hair look tousled, as if you've just got out of bed – yes, that's it.'

Then she grabbed June's hand and began pulling her along the corridor.

'Ow!' groaned June, stumbling, as her ankle began to hurt once more. 'Careful, Bonnie! I've twisted my ankle.'

'Golly!' said Bonnie. 'How did you do that?'

'Fell off my bicycle,' said June, glumly. 'And it was all a waste of time, for no one turned up. But never mind that! I want to know what has been going on here.'

Bonnie told her as they walked, and June came to a halt suddenly.

'So, *you* solved the mystery after all,' she said in rather a small voice.

'No, I didn't!' said Bonnie. '*You* were the one who worked out that our blank piece of paper wasn't blank, after all. Without knowing that, we wouldn't have got anywhere. I simply guessed that it was a ruse to get Bill and Clarissa out of the way. So, you see, June, we *both* played a part. It was teamwork!'

'So it was!' said June, looking brighter. 'Well, I'm beginning to think that there's rather a lot to be said for teamwork!'

'I'm glad to hear it,' said Bonnie, with a smile. 'Now, do come along, or the Head will start thinking that we have run away! Oh, and you will have to try and hide your limp. Miss Grayling will never believe that you twisted your ankle lying in bed.'

'I'll do my best,' said June, wincing. They were outside Miss Grayling's door now, and she said to Bonnie, 'Is there anything else I should know, before we go in?'

'Oh yes,' said Bonnie, tapping at the door. 'The police are inside and they want to interview both of us.'

It was the early hours of the morning by the time Felicity, June and Bonnie got to bed. By that time, the whole dormitory was awake, for Bonnie had accidentally bumped into Esme's bed when she slipped in to fetch June's night-clothes. Bonnie had disappeared by the time Esme was fully awake, and the girl had lain there for a moment, wondering what had disturbed her. Then she sat up and, as her eyes became accustomed to the darkness, she spotted the three empty beds, and gave an involuntary cry of alarm. This roused the others, of course, and they stared at the empty beds in astonishment, quite unable to imagine what could have happened to the three absentees.

'Surely they haven't all gone off somewhere together!' said Amy, rather put out that she hadn't been taken into Bonnie's confidence.

'Well, if they haven't, it's a bit of a coincidence,' said Susan, who was also feeling rather hurt that Felicity had gone off somewhere without her.

'I know some of the South Tower girls were talking about a midnight feast,' said Freddie. 'Do you suppose they have been invited to that?' But if that was so, why hadn't June invited her along too, she thought, feeling rather left out.

Pam shook her head decidedly, and said, 'You know that there is a strict rule about girls leaving their tower to go to another, after lights-out. June and Freddie might break it, but Felicity *never* would.'

'No, she wouldn't,' said Susan, her brow clearing a little.

'Perhaps they're hiding somewhere, and playing a trick on us!' suggested Nora.

'Yes, that's it!' cried Freddie. 'I'll bet they are all in the bathroom, listening like anything, and laughing their heads off at us!'

And Freddie had leapt out of bed and run to the bathroom, pulling open the door. But, of course, it was empty.

'Where *can* they be?' asked Freddie, scratching her head.

There was a good deal of speculation, until the three girls themselves walked in. First Felicity, then Bonnie, and then June, who was limping quite badly now. They were immediately pounced on by the others. And what a tale they had to tell!

The note *had* been intended as a diversion. When the police – alerted by Bonnie – arrived at Five Oaks, they had caught Mr Banks and several of his grooms in the act of letting the horses out.

'And then they planned to set fire to the stable block!' said Bonnie. 'Did you ever hear of anything so wicked?'

'The police got there in the nick of time,' explained Felicity. 'Of course, Mr Banks and his accomplices were arrested, and they admitted being behind all the unpleasant happenings at Five Oaks.'

'Yes, it seems that Eleanor's uncle wanted to buy Five Oaks for himself,' said June. 'But he knew that the girls would never sell willingly, and set about trying to put them out of business, so that they would have no choice in the matter.'

'Mr Banks! Who would have thought it?'

'And we all thought that he was being so kind to Bill and Clarissa, when all the time it was an act!'

'You said that he looked sinister, Felicity,' said Susan. 'And you were right!'

Julie had sat pale and silent as the tale unfolded, for, exciting as it was, there was only one thought in her head. With a flicker of hope in her eyes, she looked at the three girls now, and said, 'What about Jack?'

'That's the best news of all!' said June happily. 'Jack is safe and well! The police found him stabled at Mr Banks's. He has been well looked after, and not ill-treated in any way. They took him straight back to Five Oaks, so you can go over and visit him tomorrow.'

There was silence for a moment, then a rousing cheer went up. Suddenly everyone went mad, jumping up and down on the beds, and clapping one another on the back. Lucy hugged Julie so hard that the two of them almost over-balanced, while Nora did a little tap dance in the middle of the floor!

'June and Bonnie, I simply can't thank you enough!' said a grateful Julie, her face shining with happiness. 'I just wish there was some way I could repay you! If there's ever anything I can do for either of you, anything at all, you have only to say the word!'

'You're a real pair of heroines,' said Lucy. 'Three cheers for June and Bonnie!'

And, once again, the third formers cheered for all they were worth, while June and Bonnie turned red and beamed with pride.

'Oh, how I wish I could go and see my darling Jack right this very minute!' said Julie longingly.

'Well, you're just going to have to be patient!' laughed Felicity. 'I've had quite enough excitement for one night, thank you.'

'Sandy will keep an eye on Jack for you tonight, old girl,' said Lucy, clapping her friend on the shoulder. 'He will be so glad to have his old friend back!'

Julie's expression grew serious suddenly, and she said bitterly, 'Eleanor must have known where Jack was all along. And she pretended to feel sorry for me. The beast!'

'Yes, what part *did* dear Eleanor play in all this?' asked Amy.

'Well, she was in on the plan to drive Bill and Clarissa out, of course,' said Bonnie, taking up the story. 'It was she who stole Bill and Clarissa's cash-box, on her uncle's orders.'

'I always knew that Eleanor was mean, but I didn't think that even she would stoop so low,' said Pam in disgust.

'Apparently, Mr Banks told the police that Eleanor tried to talk him out of stealing Jack,' said Felicity. 'But he had made his mind up. And she had no idea that he had planned to burn the stables down tonight. It was Eleanor who wrote the note that Bonnie found in Jack's stable, but she really believed that her uncle was going to hand Jack over to Bill and Clarissa tonight.'

'We saw her, briefly, after the police had spoken to her,' said June, sounding very serious, for once. 'They must have been quite hard on her, for she looked simply dreadful, and very shaken indeed.'

'I'd jolly well like to shake her, all right!' said Lucy, harshly. 'Perhaps she didn't know all of her uncle's plans, but she *did* know that he was up to no good – and she went along with it.'

'Of course, Miss Grayling isn't going to keep her here,' said Felicity. 'She is to leave tomorrow, and go to live with her aunt until her parents are back in the country.'

'So she'll still be nearby,' said Nora in disgust.

'Not for long, I don't suppose,' said June. 'I should think that Mrs Banks will want to sell up and move away, for the shame will be too much to bear once word gets around that her husband is an out-and-out villain!'

'Bill and Clarissa must be awfully bucked,' said Pam. 'They won't have to sell Five Oaks after all.'

'Yes, they arrived home just as Mr Banks was being arrested,' said Bonnie. 'Of course, Bill's brothers were all for dealing with him themselves, Sergeant Dobbs said, but the police wouldn't allow it.'

'Pity,' said Nora, with a sigh. 'I daresay they would have taught him a lesson he wouldn't forget in a hurry.'

'And Sergeant Dobbs also said that Mr Banks will have to pay the girls compensation, for all the damage he has done to their property and their reputation,' Felicity said happily. 'So that's jolly good as well.'

June and Bonnie's interview with the police had been a much more pleasant experience than Eleanor's. Sergeant Dobbs and his colleagues had been most impressed with their detective work, and had praised the two girls quite extravagantly.

'Well, it's no more than you deserve,' said Julie, when the girls recounted this.

'I'll say!' agreed Esme. 'My goodness, what a night it's been!'

'Yes, it's just a pity that we missed most of the excitement,' said Nora.

'Well, I missed most of it too, as it turned out,' said June, with a comical expression. 'For I spent most of the night sitting up a tree, and ended up falling off a bicycle!'

The others roared with laughter at this, and at last Felicity said, 'I was going to tick you off properly for sneaking out, June. But everything has turned out so well, and I feel so happy, that I just can't be angry with you any more.'

'I should jolly well think not!' said June, putting on an enormous air of self-importance. 'After all, I *am* a heroine! Besides, I've punished myself already; for my ankle is going to be black and blue tomorrow.'

'Golly, yes, your poor ankle!' said Freddie. 'We shall have to think up a story to account for that.'

'Perhaps you can pretend to slip on your way downstairs tomorrow,' said Susan, with a yawn.

'Tomorrow? You mean today,' said Pam, looking at her alarm clock. 'It's almost three o'clock!'

'Heavens!' said Felicity. 'We have to be up in a few hours, and I suddenly feel worn out. I shall never be able to do it.'

Just then they heard the sound of footsteps outside the dormitory, and then the door opened and Miss Grayling herself stood there. It was a most unusual occurrence for the Head to visit one of the dormitories, and the girls stopped talking at once, all of them looking rather sheepish. Gracious, they must have been making a frightful din to have brought Miss Grayling on the scene! But the headmistress's blue eyes twinkled, and she said, 'It's all right, girls, I haven't come to tell you off, for I realise that this has been no ordinary night. In fact, it has been quite *extra*ordinary!'

The girls smiled at this, and the Head went on, 'I know that you have all had a lot to talk about, and no doubt feel thoroughly overexcited, but I really must insist that you get to sleep now.'

'But, Miss Grayling, if I drop off now I shall never wake up in time for breakfast,' protested June. 'Can't we go to bed early tonight, instead?'

'No, June,' said the Head firmly. 'Once you close your eyes, I think you will find that you are a lot more tired than you realise. All of you, into bed at once, please.'

The third formers obeyed immediately, for most of

them really did feel very tired and were secretly quite glad to be ordered into bed.

'Now, I don't want another sound from this dormitory until the dressing-bell rings,' said the Head, turning off the light. Then she stood quite still for a moment, silhouetted in the doorway. 'There is just one more thing that I need to say to you, June, and to Bonnie,' she said softly. 'I am very, very proud of both of you.'

And with that, Miss Grayling closed the door gently, and the third formers heard her footsteps fading away into the distance.

'Well!' whispered Freddie. 'Fancy the Grayling saying *that*! I bet that you're as pleased as punch, aren't you, June? June?'

But there was no answer, for Miss Grayling had been quite right. June was fast asleep.

A surprise for June

Felicity, June, Bonnie and Nora all found it quite impossible to get out of bed the following morning.

'Though I don't know why *Nora* should be so tired,' said Esme, looking down at the sleeping girl. 'She didn't have an adventure last night, like the other three did.'

'Nora can *never* get out of bed in the morning,' laughed Pam, bending down to give her friend a shake. 'Come on, sleeping beauty! Wakey wakey!'

Nora opened her eyes a fraction, mumbled something that no one could understand, then turned over and promptly went back to sleep again.

'There's only one thing for it,' said Pam. 'We shall have to pull the covers off her.'

And Pam and Esme did just that, causing Nora to sit up angrily and shake her fist at them.

But no one quite liked to dish out the same treatment to the other three who were still asleep. If anyone had earned a lie-in, they had!

Just then, though, Felicity opened her eyes, lying quite still for a few seconds as the events of the previous night came back to her. For a moment she thought that it had all been a strange dream, but then she saw Julie, chattering happily to Lucy, a beaming smile on her face, and she knew that it had really happened. Julie would not look so happy if her beloved Jack were still missing.

Bonnie began to stir too, then June, and just as the three girls were thinking about getting out of bed, Matron bustled in.

'Come along, you third formers!' she chivvied them. 'There will be no breakfast left for you, if you don't get a move on.'

'I say, Matron,' said Pam. 'We shan't have to face Eleanor in the dining-room, shall we?'

'Indeed you shan't!' said Matron grimly. 'Her aunt will be along to fetch her very shortly, and until she arrives, Eleanor will stay in her dormitory, out of the way.'

Privately, Matron thought that it would have done Eleanor the world of good to have to face the scorn and hard stares of the others, but the girl was far too weak to do that. She would never be able to look at any of the Malory Towers girls again!

Felicity swung her legs over the edge of the bed, and Matron said, 'Not you, Felicity! Or June, or Bonnie. Miss Grayling has given orders that you are to have breakfast in bed today.'

The three girls looked at one another in delight, and Nora called out hopefully, 'Can I have breakfast in bed too, Matron?'

'No, you jolly well can't!' cried Matron, trying her best to look stern, though her eyes twinkled. 'In fact, if you don't finish getting dressed this minute,

Nora, you'll be on bread and water.'

Muttering darkly, Nora quickly dressed, and followed the rest of her form downstairs, leaving the other three alone.

'Breakfast in bed!' sighed June contentedly, propping her pillow up behind her and snuggling into it. 'What a treat!'

And soon the girls were tucking into big bowls of creamy porridge, followed by fluffy, scrambled eggs and buttered toast, all washed down with big mugs of tea.

'Yummy!' said Felicity, spreading marmalade on a piece of toast. 'But my goodness, how these crumbs do get into the bedclothes!'

'The secret is to hold the plate right under your chin,' said Bonnie, demonstrating. 'Gosh, this marmalade is simply delicious! I don't know why breakfast always tastes so much nicer when it's eaten in bed, but there's no doubt that it does!'

The girls ate in silence for a few moments, then June said, 'Everything is going to feel a bit flat now, after all the excitement yesterday.'

'Oh, I don't know,' said Felicity. 'There is still the tennis tournament with St Margarets to look forward to.'

'So there is!' said June, sounding more cheerful. 'With everything that has happened lately, I had almost forgotten about that.'

Then her face fell and she cried, 'Oh, my goodness! There's something else I'd forgotten about – my ankle! Suppose it's not healed in time for me to play?'

'Have you looked at it this morning?' asked Bonnie. 'Perhaps it will be better now.'

June put her breakfast tray aside and gingerly pulled back the covers – then all three girls gasped. Far from being better, June's ankle had swollen up dreadfully, and was quite horribly bruised.

'Oh, June!' said Felicity, in dismay. 'That looks awfully painful.'

'Well, I can't feel it at all while I'm just lying here,' said June. 'But I expect it will be painful when I try to stand.'

'You had better arrange to have a little accident before Matron sees it,' said Bonnie. 'She'll be back to take our breakfast trays away soon.'

'I know!' cried Felicity. 'Go into the bathroom, and you can pretend that you've slipped on the soap. Hurry, for I think I can hear Matron coming!'

Trying not to put any weight on her ankle, June carefully got out of bed and hopped into the bathroom. She shut the door behind her just as Matron came into the dormitory.

'All finished?' she asked. 'Good! I'm pleased to see that last night's little adventure hasn't affected your appetites. But where is June?'

Before either of the girls could answer, there came the sound of a crash from the bathroom, followed by a squeal.

'Ow!' yelled June. 'Do help me, someone! I've hurt myself.'

Felicity and Bonnie were out of their beds in a flash, but Matron reached the bathroom before them.

'Goodness me!' she exclaimed, throwing open the door. 'What on earth have you done to yourself, June?'

'Someone dropped a bar of soap on the floor, Matron, and I slipped on it,' said June, who was half-sitting, half-lying on the floor, her face screwed up in pain most convincingly. 'I seem to have twisted my ankle.'

Matron crouched down beside the injured girl and rolled up her pyjama leg a little way.

'You certainly *have* twisted it!' she said. 'Quite badly, by the look of it. Normally the swelling and bruising don't come out for a good few hours,' she added, looking hard at June.

She stood up and helped June to her feet, saying, 'You'd better come along to the San with me, my girl, and get it bandaged up.'

Then Matron turned to Felicity and Bonnie, who were hovering by the bathroom door, saying briskly, 'Get dressed, please, girls, and go to your first lesson. Explain to Miss Peters what has happened, and tell her that I will send June along as soon as I have finished with her.'

'Yes, Matron,' chorused the two girls, trying not to laugh as June winked at them behind Matron's back.

Matron helped June to get dressed, then insisted that the girl lean on her on the way to the San. Their progress was impeded, as they ran into several girls on the way, all of whom wanted to congratulate June for the part she had played in reuniting Jack with his mistress, putting things right for Bill and Clarissa, and bringing Mr Banks to justice.

'Jolly good show, June!'

'You deserve a medal.'

'Yes, a lot of people have reason to be grateful to you and Bonnie, June.'

Matron, knowing that June deserved their congratulations, bore with this patiently. But her patience was at an end when Mam'zelle Dupont suddenly appeared and, spotting June, tottered over on her high heels.

'Ah, this brave and clever June!' she cried. 'Matron, this girl is to be applauded! If it was not for her, and the dear Bonnie, the evil Mr Banks might have got away with his so-wicked plan.'

'I am well aware of that, Mam'zelle,' said Matron crisply. 'But I really must get June to the San, for she has injured her ankle.'

'*Mon dieu!*' exclaimed Mam'zelle, looking shocked. 'How did this happen? June, were you injured performing some act of bravery, or bringing some desperate villain to justice?'

'No, Mam'zelle,' said Matron impatiently. 'She slipped on the soap.'

And, leaving Mam'zelle to gaze after them in astonishment, she bore June off to the San. There she bandaged her ankle up very tightly, and very efficiently.

'You are to rest it completely,' she instructed, in a tone that invited no argument. 'Keep the foot up as much as possible and, with a bit of luck, you should be as right as rain in a few weeks.'

A few weeks! The tennis tournament took place in three weeks, and June was absolutely determined that her ankle would be healed by then and she would be able to play.

There was another surprise for June and Bonnie when Bill and Clarissa arrived at Malory Towers halfway through the morning. Miss Peters, most surprisingly, allowed them to interrupt her lesson so that they could thank June and Bonnie in front of the whole form.

'But for you two, we might have had to sell Five Oaks,' said Bill gratefully. 'We simply can't thank you enough.'

'We can't afford to give you a reward,' said Clarissa. 'But the two of you can have free horse rides whenever you want.'

Bonnie, who was no horsewoman, didn't look awfully thrilled at this, though she appreciated the spirit in which the offer was made. June, though, was quite delighted, and cried, 'I shall take you up on that – once my beastly ankle is all right!'

Alas for June, she was not a good invalid! It chafed her to watch the others splashing around in the swimming-pool, or playing tennis, while she could only sit and watch. It drove her mad when Freddie and Nora had a pillow fight in the dormitory one night and, instead of taking part, she was a mere spectator. And the hardest thing of all to bear was when the third formers decided to have a picnic at the foot of Langley Hill.

Langley Hill was a popular beauty spot, and the girls were thrilled when Miss Peters suggested that they have a picnic tea there one day.

'Super!' said Felicity. 'Cook is going to make us some sandwiches and sausage rolls to take with us. Susan and I are going to provide the ginger beer.'

'And I have a tin of biscuits in my locker that Mother sent,' said Pam. 'I'll bring those.'

All of the girls agreed to bring something along to the picnic, except for June, who remained oddly glum and silent.

'Anything up, old girl?' asked Freddie, concerned. 'Aren't you looking forward to the picnic?'

'I shan't be coming to the picnic,' said June in a tight little voice. 'Langley Hill is a good half hour's walk away, and my ankle will never stand it.'

'Oh, June!' cried Freddie in dismay. 'I never thought of that! Well, I shan't go to the picnic either, then. The two of us will stay at Malory Towers and do something together.'

But June would not hear of this. 'No, I don't want to spoil your fun,' she said, trying to sound like her usual, carefree self.

But Freddie wasn't fooled for a minute. And nor was Julie, who overheard this. An idea came to her suddenly. She was very much in June's debt, and she was going to repay that debt by making sure that June joined in the picnic.

Julie, of course, was absolutely thrilled to have Jack back, and had spent every spare moment over at Five Oaks.

'Almost as if she's afraid to let him out of her sight!' as Pam said to Nora.

Julie wasn't afraid, for now that Mr Banks was out of the way, she knew that Jack was not in any danger. But she had missed him quite dreadfully, and wanted to make up for lost time. But she wasn't so wrapped up in Jack that she couldn't spare a thought for anyone else – especially June, to whom she owed so much.

She took the others into her confidence and, on

Saturday afternoon, when they were in the common-room, Felicity said to June, 'Do hurry up! We're going to leave for Langley Hill in a few minutes.'

'I told you, I'm not coming to Langley Hill,' said June rather crossly. 'How can I?'

Felicity exchanged a glance with Freddie, who nodded. Then the two girls each grabbed one of June's arms, hauling her up out of her chair.

'Hey!' cried June, bewildered. 'What do you think you're doing?'

'We're taking you on a picnic,' laughed Freddie.

Between them, the two girls managed to get June outside. And there, waiting for her, was Julie, leading Jack.

'I've organised some transport for you, June,' said Julie, with a grin. 'All you have to do is sit on Jack's back, and he will carry you to Langley Hill. I'll hold his reins, so that he doesn't take it into his head to gallop off with you, or anything.'

June was speechless for a moment – a most unusual thing for her. Then her face broke into a broad smile, and she cried, 'My word, what a picnic this is going to be!'

And indeed it was. The girls feasted on sandwiches, sausage rolls, cake, biscuits – and all kinds of goodies. Then they lazed around drinking ginger beer, chatting and telling jokes. It was a very happy day. But, all too soon, it was time to clear up and make their way back to school.

'Thank you, Julie,' said June, as the girl helped her up into the saddle. Then she leaned forward and patted

Jack's neck. 'And thank you, Jack. I've had a simply marvellous time!'

'It really has been a nice day,' said Felicity to Susan, when the girls arrived back at Malory Towers. 'No quarrels, no unpleasant shocks, no excitement – just a lovely, peaceful time. Just what we all needed after everything that has happened lately.'

The girls were in the common-room that evening when a second former put her head round the door and called out, 'I say! Miss Grayling wants to see Esme Walters in her study.'

'Goodness, not more trouble!' said Susan. 'What does Miss Grayling want with you, Esme?'

But Esme didn't have the slightest idea, and went off to the Head's study feeling mystified and a little worried. Whatever could the Head want to see her about?

A lovely end to the term

'Come in!' called out Miss Grayling, as Esme knocked timidly on her door. Looking rather scared, Esme went in, but the Head was smiling as she invited Esme to sit down.

'Esme,' she began, 'I have been speaking to Miss Peters, and she tells me that your work has improved a great deal as the term has gone on. Miss Hibbert and both the Mam'zelles are very pleased with you too. Now that you have settled down and learned to work hard, you are far ahead of most of the third formers in many subjects.'

Esme turned quite red with pleasure and said, 'Well, I really have been trying my hardest, Miss Grayling.'

'That is quite obvious,' said the Head. 'And your hard work has paid off. You see, Esme, you are quite a bit older than the rest of your form. Starting off in the third form was only ever meant to be temporary, until we saw what you could do. And Miss Peters agrees with me that, next term, when the others go up into the fourth form, you should go up into the fifth.'

Esme was so astonished that she couldn't utter a word! Her feelings were rather mixed. On the one hand, it was a great honour to go up into the fifth form next term, and her parents would be absolutely delighted with her. But she would miss the others quite dreadfully – Lucy, Bonnie, Amy, Felicity and the rest.

Almost as if she could read the girl's thoughts, Miss Grayling said, 'Of course, I understand that you will miss your cousin, and the friends that you have made. But, although you won't be in the same form any longer, you will still be able to see them.'

'Yes,' said Esme. 'But friendships aren't quite the same if you are in different forms.'

'True,' said Miss Grayling. 'But there will be new girls for you to meet, and new friendships to make.'

That sounded exciting, and Esme felt a little cheered as she returned to the common-room to tell the others her news.

The third formers, too, had mixed feelings, for although they were thrilled for Esme, they would have liked her to stay with them. She really had changed a lot as the term went on, and since she had stopped trying to copy Amy, her own natural, very likeable personality had shone through.

Felicity and Susan's shouts of, 'Good for you, Esme!' mingled with Bonnie's plaintive, 'Oh, I shall miss you so much, Esme!'

'And I will miss all of you,' said Esme. 'Though I feel terribly pleased that Miss Grayling thinks that I'm good enough to go up into the fifth.'

'I don't suppose you will want anything to do with us next term,' said Freddie, with a laugh. 'You'll go all high-and-mighty on us, I expect!'

'Never!' said Esme. Then she turned to Lucy and said, 'Well, cousin, just as we've made friends again, it looks as if we're about to be split up.'

'Of course we aren't, silly!' said Lucy. 'We shall still be able to have the holidays together – and I shall expect my fifth-form cousin to look after me next term!'

'I'll jolly well take you under my wing, all right!' said Esme, and the others laughed.

'You sounded quite English for a moment, there, Esme,' said June. 'Another term, and I think your American accent will be gone completely.'

'Well, I don't know if I will ever lose it completely,' said Esme. 'I quite enjoy being a bit of a mixture, to be honest. But I have come to see that there are a lot of good things about being an English schoolgirl. Why, I'm even looking forward to learning how to play lacrosse next term!'

This was going too far for Amy, who uttered a faint murmur of protest, but Felicity clapped Esme on the back and said, 'Well, if you do as well at lacrosse as you have done at tennis, you'll be just fine!'

'Speaking of tennis,' said Pam, 'do you think that you will be able to play in the tournament, June?'

'Yes, of course,' said June, with more confidence than she felt. 'Matron says that I should be able to take the bandage off next week, and as long as I take things slowly for a few days, everything should be all right.'

When the time came for the bandage to be removed, it was difficult to read Matron's expression. She prodded June's ankle gently, 'hmm-ing' and 'aah-ing' a good deal.

Poor June grew quite nervous. Surely she couldn't have done any serious damage – could she?

But, at last, Matron said, 'It's healing very nicely. The bruise has almost disappeared, and the swelling has gone down quite a bit. All the same, I don't want you doing anything too strenuous for a while, June, or you'll set yourself back.'

'Yes, Matron,' said June in a meek voice that didn't fool Matron at all!

Then she went off to the tennis court, to find Amanda Chartelow. The sixth former was playing a practice game against one of her friends and, as she watched, June marvelled again that someone who was normally so ungainly could be so graceful and lovely to watch when she played tennis.

Amanda spotted June as she came off the court, and went across to her.

'Ah, you've had your bandage off!' she said, looking pleased. 'Did Matron say that you will be fit to play against St Margarets?'

'As long as I take things easy in the meantime,' said June. 'Which is exactly what I intend to do, for I badly want to play in the match.'

This was just what Amanda liked to hear, and she clapped June on the back, saying, 'That's the spirit! All the same, June, if there's the slightest doubt in your mind about whether you are fit to play, I would rather you told me. I'm going all out to win this tournament.'

And, although she was quite fed up with watching the

others all have the fun, June stuck to her word and didn't do anything that might strain her ankle for the next week or so.

Two days before the tournament, she said to Amanda, 'I really think it would be as well if I practised a little today. It seems like absolutely ages since I last played tennis.'

'Yes, I suppose that would be an idea,' said Amanda. 'And it will be a good way of testing if your ankle really is up to the strain. Go and have a game with Freddie.'

So June found the ever-willing Freddie, and the two of them took their places on the court. She and Freddie played pat-ball at first, just to get June used to swinging her racket again. But June soon grew impatient with this, and said, 'That's enough! Let's play properly, Freddie – and no going easy on me!'

Freddie took June at her word, and a couple of fiercely fought games ensued. Then June ran forward to return one of Freddie's serves, and suddenly her ankle just seemed to give way. She stumbled, but didn't fall. And, although June managed to stop herself crying out in pain, she winced.

'What's up?' called Freddie, walking up to the net. 'Oh! Don't say that your ankle's given out.'

'No such thing!' said June, determined to play on. 'I just tripped, that's all. Serve again, Freddie!'

Freddie did, and no one would have been able to tell from June's manner that she was in pain. True, her game was a little off, but Freddie put that down to the fact that she was out of practice. June even managed to laugh and joke with Freddie as the two of them walked off to the changing-rooms, but how relieved she was to be able to sit down on one of the benches in there and take the weight off her ankle. Blow! she thought. If only she had listened to Bonnie and not gone to Bluebell Wood that fateful night, she would never have fallen off that beastly bike. Now what was she to do?

It didn't take June long to decide. She *would* play in the tournament! And she would jolly well do her best to win. Why, when people learned afterwards that she had played with a badly hurt ankle, they would simply praise her to the skies!

So it came about that, when the Malory Towers team gathered on the drive to wait for the coach that was to take them to St Margarets, June was among them.

As usual, Amanda gave the team a little pep talk while they were waiting.

'I want you all to do your best, for the honour of Malory Towers,' she said. 'No one can ask more of you than that. If you play as well as you possibly can, and lose, I shall still be proud of you. But woe betide anyone who doesn't try her very hardest!'

The girls stood straight and proud, all of them looking very smart in their white tennis dresses and cardigans, as they listened to their captain. Each and every one of them felt determined not to let their school down. But June looked rather pensive. Amanda's words had given her food for thought. How could she possibly play her best, and try her hardest, when she simply wasn't up to it? She was letting Malory Towers down just by taking her place on the team – a place that should be taken by someone who really *could* give of her best. Taking a deep breath, June went up to the games captain and said, 'Amanda! There's something I need to tell you. You see, my ankle isn't really better at all. I thought that it was, and when I realised it wasn't I kept quiet, because I so badly wanted to play in the tournament. I see now, though, that the best thing I can do for Malory Towers is to stand aside and let someone else play.'

Amanda stared hard at June for a moment. She looked very stern, and June waited for the storm to break over her head. Then Amanda's face broke into a smile and she said gruffly, 'Good kid! I know it must have cost you a great deal to give up your place on the team, but you have done the right thing. I really believe that you are beginning to learn about team spirit.'

And Amanda was quite right, June suddenly realised. There were times when one had to put one's own desire for personal glory aside, for the good of others. She had first discovered that when she and Bonnie had worked side by side to find Jack, and to get Bill and Clarissa out of trouble. And it had been a lesson well learned, for when Amanda called Esme over and informed the surprised girl that she would be playing after all, June felt no bitterness or jealousy. Instead she patted Esme on the back and said heartily, 'Good luck, Esme! Make sure that you play up.'

Just then, the big coach drew up and, as June began to walk towards the school, Amanda called out, 'And just where do you think you're going, June?'

'I thought I'd go and sit in the common-room for a bit,' answered June, surprised.

'Well, think again!' said Amanda, taking her arm and steering the girl towards the coach. 'There are a couple of spare seats, so you can come with us and be our mascot. Just make sure you cheer us on, good and loud!'

'Oh, I will, Amanda,' said June happily. 'Yes, I'll do that, all right.'

And June yelled herself hoarse! Amanda won her match easily, the St Margarets girls gasping at the brilliance of her play. Poor Vanessa Tyler wasn't so lucky and, although she played her heart out, was narrowly beaten by her opponent. Then came the doubles match, and Felicity and Susan walked out on to the court, both of them feeling very proud and very nervous.

'Come on, Felicity!' shouted June. 'Come on, Susan!'

And, to the delight of June and Amanda, the two girls played superbly. Their opponents were very good too, and did their best, but they were no match for the Malory Towers pair.

'Jolly well played, kids!' shouted Amanda. 'Two–one to Malory Towers! Emily, from the fourth form, is playing next. I should think that she's certain to win.'

But alas, this was Emily's first match in front of a crowd, and her nerves overcame her completely. She made some bad mistakes, with the result that the St Margarets girl won.

'It all depends on Esme now,' said Amanda, looking

very tense. 'Her match will decide whether we go back to Malory Towers as winners or losers.'

June cheered her head off as Esme came out, a tall, graceful figure. The girl she was playing against was much more heavily built, and had a powerful serve, but a calm determination had settled on Esme, and she fought back well. The play was very even, until the last couple of games, when the Malory Towers girl really settled down and, to the delight of her team-mates, took the lead. Then it was the final game of the set, and Esme was serving for the match.

At the side of the court, June and Amanda were silent now, both of them holding their breath. Esme served beautifully, the ball whizzing across the net and sending up a little puff of chalk as it bounced off the line.

'The St Margarets girl will never reach that!' said June, clutching excitedly at Amanda's arm.

And she didn't! Game, set, match and tournament to Malory Towers!

While the girls from the other school clapped sportingly, the Malory Towers team – and June, of course – went quite mad with joy. They shouted, cheered, hugged one another and leapt up and down.

'Congratulations,' said the St Margarets captain, coming over to shake hands with Amanda. 'That's quite a team you have there!'

'Yes,' said Amanda, beaming round proudly at the girls. 'The best team ever!'

Of course, the girls got a heroes' welcome when they

returned to school, Felicity and Esme clutching the big silver cup that was the team prize between them.

'What a super end to the term!' said Pam.

'Absolutely marvellous!' agreed Freddie.

'But it's not *quite* the end of term,' said Nora. 'There are still a few days to go.'

And those few days simply sped by, and then it really *was* the end of term. The girls were plunged into the usual last-minute frenzy of packing and, in the dormitory, chaos reigned.

'Has anyone seen my slippers?'

'I say, where *has* my hairbrush got to?'

'Nora, do get your big feet off my music case!'

'Felicity! Felicity! What do you mean by going off with my pyjamas?'

'Oh, are those yours, Lucy? Sorry, they look exactly like mine.'

Matron, popping her head round the door to see how the third formers were getting on, winced as a wave of noise hit her, and clapped her hands over her ears, before quickly withdrawing again.

At last, everyone was packed and they made their way down to the big hall, where girls from all of the towers were waiting for the coaches to take them to the station, or for their parents to collect them by car. Mam'zelle Dupont was fussing round everyone, as she always did, saying fond goodbyes, and the girls smiled to see her.

'Dear old Mam'zelle,' said Susan. 'I shall miss her funny ways during the holidays.'

'I shall miss everything about Malory Towers,' said Felicity with a sigh. 'My last term as head of the form is over now. And what an eventful term it has been!'

'Yes, it's certainly had its ups and downs,' agreed Susan. 'Luckily, in the end, the ups seemed to outweigh the downs!'

'I wonder what will be in store for us next term?' said Felicity.

'Who knows?' said Susan. 'We'll just have to wait and see.'

And that's what we will have to do as well – wait and see.

Don't miss the next Malory Towers story ...

Enid Blyton

Malory Towers

Winter Term

Written by Pamela Cox

Fourth-former Susan's in charge of the winter
concert, but new teacher Miss Tallant won't
let her make any decisions. When Miss Tallant
interferes in a midnight feast, the girls realise
that there's a spy among them ...

Look out for more classic school stories from

Enid Blyton

ST CLARE'S

Schooldays at St Clare's are never dull
for twins Pat and Isabel O'Sullivan
and their friends.

There's mischief at St Clare's!